THE LAST APPOINTMENT

30 COLLECTED SHORT STORIES

CHARLES LEVIN

First Edition

ISBN: 978-1-7352108-7-2

OTHER TITLES BY CHARLES LEVIN

CONTENTS

To Josh and Dan,
my guys

PREFACE

Mysteries, thrillers, suspense, personal reflections, biases, strange twists, rants, love, death, dreams, and memories are all contained in this collection of short stories and essays written over the last few years—pre-, post-, and during the pandemic.

The title story, *The Last Appointment*, is brand new and has never been published elsewhere. Some stories have appeared on my blog and others have disappeared from that ephemeral space.

Most of the stories are short reads, which pretty much matches my attention span. Feel free to open the collection anywhere and cherry-pick at will, although I do recommend you read the first story first. It will give you a flavor for what's to come and maybe put you in a magical frame of mind.

Otherwise, the experience of reading these stories is up to you. After publishing four full-length novels and spending time with some of my readers, I found that everyone brings their own life experiences to bear and embraces or reacts to stories in their own very personal way. Some aspects of these tales may resonate with you and others will blow by or even repel you.

Whatever your experience, know that my primary mission is to entertain and then maybe ask or tease you with some big questions. Personally, I enjoy reading for fun, but it always adds more to my enjoyment when I can learn something along the way.

Years ago, I remember watching an episode of that warm and folksy travelogue, *On The Road, with Charles Kuralt.* He captured endearing tales of ordinary people doing extraordinary things all across America. Over twenty years starting in 1967, he stopped in every state with his CBS bus and interviewed a diverse group of people. I was quite young at the time, but I was struck by one particular interview. He spoke with an undereducated man who had taught himself to read and over decades amassed an extensive library. It was somewhere in the South. I tried to track down the details, but this was pre-YouTube and pre-Internet. If you can find that episode, let me know.

Anyway, in the man's modest home, Kuralt asks this avid reader and book collector how he reads. The man answers that he is a very slow reader because, "I likes to ponders as I reads." Being a slow reader myself, I could identify with that.

So I hope you will slow down, enjoy, and ponder as you read *The Last Appointment.*

– Charles Levin, November 2021

PART I

FICTION

THE LAST APPOINTMENT

"I n my twenty-five years of practice, I have never…" Lark says.

Dr. Saul Geier looks at his former student, long since an accomplished psychiatrist. He studies her unkempt, auburn hair and the powdered whiteness of her complexion interrupted by swollen hazel eyes. Then, he turns his gaze out the floor-to-ceiling windows of his tenth-story office on Fifth Avenue. "We've known each other for a long time, Susan. We used to discuss cases often until you surpassed your mentor. I don't take it personally. It's a point of pride for me that you've done so well. But why, after ten years, come to me now?"

Susan Lark clenches her fists and sucks in a deep breath. "It's not only that I'm stumped, which I am, but I might be losing my mind too. I didn't know who else to turn to."

Geier's face seems to smile with wrinkles, his blue eyes piercing. "You probably didn't know since we lost touch, but I'm retiring today. I think at age ninety-two it's finally time to hang it up. I don't know how many patients I've seen over the last sixty years, but most are gone now. I think what I'll miss most is this view of the city, the four seasons over Central Park, the blossoms in the spring, the winter snow blanketing the ponds and meadows, the bikers and joggers and baby carriages, the hawks and geese taking a rest stop during their southbound fall journey. I have relished the seasons of life right here."

"I'm sorry to hear that. You did a lot of good over the years, and not just for your patients. I don't know where I'd be now without your guidance and your wisdom."

Geier takes out a pouch of Captain Black and taps some tobacco into his Stanwell. He hangs the pipe unlit from the corner of his mouth. He promised his wife he would quit smoking. So for him, the smell of fresh tobacco is the next best thing.

"It's nice to hear you say that, but I'm tired. I look forward to sitting out on my deck in Montauk and staring out over the waves, inhaling the salt air. That's enough for me now. But my door will always be open to you. It just won't be here. OK, so tell me about this case."

Susan hands Geier the patient's intake form. He reads the form aloud to himself. "Anxiety, depression, sleep changes, racing thoughts, gets exercise running. She's a writer—nothing terribly unusual here. Let me see your notes."

Susan's face flushes. "I can't do that."

"Why not? You know I'll keep them confidential."

"I destroyed them."

"What? You can't do that. It's a cardinal sin—you could lose your license for that."

"I know that, but I couldn't risk someone ever reading them."

Geier rubs his fingers through his thin gray hair. "OK, then just tell me what's going on."

Susan stands and walks to the window. "You're right, it's a glorious view. You can see Central Park and all of Upper Manhattan from here." She turns back and points at the intake form. "About a month ago, that patient walked into my office. I had an immediate visceral reaction to her appearance. Yes, she was attractive, mid-forties, slender, and with a confident posture. My reaction was not sexual. Maybe it was her haunting black eyes that seemed to go right through me. As if she's known me all my life, but we'd never met before. It was eerie."

"OK, you'd already lost your objectivity, I see. It happens."

"Yes, but aren't we supposed to observe everything about our patients, especially appearance and body language?"

"It's a fine line, isn't it? Go on."

Susan looks up as if reading something on the ceiling. "Angela Auger was a writer. She wrote fiction, thrillers."

"You're using the past tense. Is she dead or just no longer a patient?"

"I'll get to that. Anyway, she tells me a story about her writing that gets more and more disturbing, bizarre really."

Geier looks back at the form. "I know this name. I believe I read a few of her books."

"You probably have. She was very talented; a few of her novels made the bestseller lists. I think her greatest knack was making her readers want to turn the page. Once you started one of her books, you couldn't put it down. Like me with potato chips and romance novels."

"That was my experience." He looks down at the end of his pipe and gives it a tap as if stoking the unlit flame. "For me, the equivalent is apple cider donuts. Sorry, continue. So she was a good writer. I'm not seeing the problem yet."

Susan sweeps the tangled hair from her eyes, then recounts the plot from one of Auger's novels. "Here's the plot from one of her recent novels. The villain, a foreign terrorist, genetically engineers a virus that turns into a pandemic. She then aligns herself with a white nationalist group that successfully pulls off a domestic terror attack on the U.S. Capitol. Sound familiar?"

Geier dumps the tobacco from his pipe in the trash and refills it. "Sure, those things happened and she wrote about them. So what?"

"You don't get it. She wrote about those things *before* they happened. Like she foresaw them. The real pandemic started just as her book was hitting the store shelves and the attack on the Capitol happened a few months later. As her fictional scenarios unfolded in the real world, that's when her anxiety attacks started. She couldn't reconcile whether she had an unusual power to predict disasters or if it was purely an accident."

"Go on," Geier says.

"When the weight of these events hit her, she stopped writing for a few months. But to Angela, writing was like breathing—she had to do it or she would die. So tentatively, she started again. She wrote a short story about an assassination attempt on the First Lady that included a scene where a bomb exploded at Union Station. Even before her editor reviewed it, both things happened. She became paralyzed by her own thoughts, fearful of writing them down."

"You are familiar with schizoaffective disorder, which might explain her delusional belief that she could see the future?"

"I am, and it was the first thing that occurred to me. Still, her delusions went a treacherous step further. She came to believe that not only did she have the power to predict the future, but she in fact was writing the future—that what she wrote caused those horrible things to happen."

"In layman's terms, a God complex."

"There's only one problem with your analysis."

"Which is?"

"I believe or should say, *believed* her."

"What made you swallow that besides her telling you those things?"

"OK, first, I read her book, *Not So Done*, and the publishing date coincided with the predictions of the pandemic and the subsequent assault on the Capitol. Those could just have been coincidences. So I gently challenged her to give me more examples." Susan sits back down, more like collapses into the chair on the other side of Geier's oversized mahogany desk. She silently looks into Geier's sympathetic eyes.

He breaks the silence. "Did she give you more examples?"

"She did. At our next session, she brought a handwritten notebook. She writes all her story ideas, notes, and first drafts in longhand. She claimed the act of writing by hand helped her think and tap into her unconscious." Susan hesitates, choking back her words.

"Would you like some water?" Geier offers.

"Sure, yes."

Geier swivels around to a mini-fridge in the credenza behind him, extracting a bottle of Poland Springs. The bottle is surprisingly cold. He rubs his palms together as he watches her take two gulps, her eyes closed.

She licks her lips. "The patient pointed me to a passage that described a twenty-four car pile-up during a snowstorm on Route 78 in Pennsylvania. People were trapped in their cars for twenty-four hours or more. She was working on a survival story about two people trapped upside down in a minivan during that storm and accident—how they relived their lives and their upside-down turbulent relationship. The couple is ultimately rescued and their lives changed for the better, their love for each other renewed as a result of the trauma they faced and overcame together. Three other people died in that accident."

"And…"

"She had a date next to the title of the story, *Two for the Road*, January 17th. Then she handed me two press clippings. The first was from the *Morning Call* dated January 20th that recounted details of the snowstorm, the accident, and the three deaths. The second story, dated February 18th in the *Modern Love* column, was written by the wife of a couple trapped in an overturned vehicle during a snowstorm that fights and ultimately reconciles while trapped for twenty-four hours in their vehicle. Auger said she felt like if she hadn't written the story, it wouldn't have happened. The three who died would be alive today."

"Hmm, extraordinary. There could be other explanations."

"Like what?"

"Like the accident or love story are still coincidences or she falsified the date of her writing either wittingly or unwittingly. People with schizoaffective disorder can do things like fabricating a date to support their delusion."

Susan steeples her fingers in front of her lips and says, "Yes, but as for the accident, according to the paper, the couple was trapped upside-down in a minivan just like Auger had written. And regarding the dates, I thumbed through her notebook and there were subsequent entries for every day leading up to the day she showed me the notebook and every day six weeks after she wrote that story. It was all too much."

Geier strokes his goatee. "I see," he says. "But she still could have faked the dates in her journal."

"Yes, I was still not a hundred percent convinced. So I thought about it and at our next session I challenged her to write down three things right there in front of me that could prove her ability to either predict, or God forgive, create the future." Susan hands Geier a piece of yellow-lined paper. Judging by the jagged top edge, it had been torn from a legal pad.

"What's this?" Geier asks.

"Read it."

Geier lowers his bifocals perched on his head and scans the document. "OK, I see a number, 30,911.40. Then there is 'trip and lose car keys,' and 'win $100.'" He slowly removes his glasses and looks up at Susan. "What's all this mean?"

Susan draws a slow breath. "Those are three *predictions* she made. The first number is the Dow Jones stock market average—"

"Don't tell me, she predicted how the stock market would close?"

"She did, for that day. Then, after her appointment, I headed out for lunch and was about to cross the street to get to my Audi. Stepping down from the curb, I stumbled. The car keys slipped from my hand and fell through a sewer grate. A sanitation worker nearby was kind enough to fish the keys out for me, but I was shaken. Still, I drove to the deli to pick up my sandwich. While paying at the checkout, I noticed the deli sold lottery tickets. I thought, *why not?*"

Geier starts wheezing. "And you won?"

Susan's words now flow in a frantic wave. "I had to believe her. After she showed me her notebook, the clippings, and the three accurate predictions, I felt like the ground was shifting under my feet. I've had dizzy spells ever since. My regular therapist was at a loss. That's why I had to see you."

"I understand. I can see how that would be troubling and make you doubt your own sanity."

Susan's face reddens. "Do you think I'm making this all up?"

"No, I think you believe what you're telling me."

"But you don't trust that this really happened?" She pauses, studying Geier's raised eyebrows. "OK then. Aside from my distress, there's one other reason I'm here."

"Oh?"

'Yes, it's the second-to-last story in her notebook. It's called, *A Knock at the Door.*"

"Wait, before you tell me that, what happened to your patient, Angela Auger?"

"Unfortunately, that's the last unfinished story in the notebook." Susan reaches into her oversized handbag. "She left this with me. Here, read the last page."

Susan hands the notebook to Geier. It's one of those composition notebooks that's black and says *School* in a white block in the middle of the cover, with white, blue-lined paper inside. The notebook is almost full. Geier turns to the last written page.

A Writer's Last Line - March 21

Main character: a midlist writer, a journeywoman, who is a journalist and a novelist on the side. Her earlier novels were science fiction. One of her heroes was Ursula Le Guin. Who says women can't write page-turning, inventive science fiction? But her fruitful imagination eventually turned to writing about things gone wrong in the actual world, more personal than political, yet still considered real-world events.

One of her novels included the detailed story of an attack on the Paris office of a satiric newspaper, similar to The Onion, *that left twelve people dead and eleven injured, followed by a bloody attack on a Jewish grocery store. Then, six months later, terrorists carried out an attack identical to the ones described in her fictional story. She freaked. How could she reconcile her story being precisely detailed and identical to what actually occurred? Had the terrorists read her story and followed it like a plan? But how could that explain the exact same number of dead and wounded?*

The writer continues to write fictional stories that come true until she eventually concludes that what she writes is not merely predicting the future but causing it. Still, she can't stop writing. She tried to stop, but then she got uncontrollable shakes and sweats, like a heroin addict in withdrawal. The pain of not writing became so severe that the only way she could get relief was to write. Yet then these terrible things happened.

Convinced that what she was writing was causing the pain and death of innocent victims, she concluded that there was only one way this story, her story, could have a happy ending. Well, not happy for her, the writer, but safer and better for the unknowing world and innocent people around her. She puts down her pen and pets her black lab, Noodles. Noodles rolls over and the writer rubs her belly. Then she gets up and walks out onto the balcony of her tenth-floor apartment on Central Park South. She looks down at the busy two-way traffic below, then out across the long expanse of Central Park. The air has an early spring feel and she could swear she smells honeysuckle. A cool breeze caresses her cheeks. A black hawk circles over a meadow in the park, riding the thermals created by the warm sun, higher and higher.

She inhales a full breath of the sweet air and jumps...

Geier's face drains of all color. He closes the notebook. "My God. did Auger actually do this, jump?"

Susan looks down at her trembling hands. "Yes, yes, she did."

The two sit quietly for a few minutes, thinking of Angela Auger. Geier considers his own fragile connections with what's real and what's not.

Finally, Susan says, "Read the second to last story."

Geier hesitates and opens the notebook again, a few pages from the end.

A Knock on the Door

Main character: an aging psychiatrist in New York. The psychiatrist made a large share of his income giving expert testimony in criminal trials. The prosecutors usually called him in when alleged murderers used an insanity defense as an explanation for the heinous crimes they committed.

The psychiatrist had evaluated hundreds of murderers who had done everything from slashing throats to decapitating their victims. The worst in his mind were those who had brutally raped and killed young children. He was called on mostly by the prosecution because he rarely concluded that the defendants were insane. He believed that in some part of their twisted minds they knew what they were doing and should be punished for their crimes. Since he had published many articles in medical journals about criminality and insanity, taught at Columbia, and been in practice for decades, his testimony in favor of the prosecution carried formidable weight with juries. So it was no surprise that jurors usually awarded life sentences or death to the killers.

One of the child-rapist-killers who had been given a life sentence was released on parole after serving twenty-two years. He had kidnapped an eight-year-old boy from a school playground, taken him to a wooded area in Central Park, penetrated him several times, and then strangled him to death.

A jogger found the child the next morning, covered in flies, a black turkey vulture feasting on the child's eyes.

The ex-con killer, now on parole, never forgot the doctor who testified so many years ago and sealed his fate, half a lifetime at Rikers. Now it was time for payback. On a warm, early spring day, the psychiatrist was in his Fifth Avenue office visiting with his last patient before his planned retirement when there was a loud knock on the door. The pounding grew louder into loud thumps and kicks....

Geier's face, now a stone-cold gray, looks up from the notebook at Susan. "Why did you bring me this?"

Tears are running down Susan's cheeks. "I had to, I had no choice."

Suddenly there is a loud thumping on his office door.

Geier shakes his head. "So we're just characters in your patient's story. Not even a story yet, just her damn notes."

Susan mutters, "Predictable, inevitable...." Her voice trails off.

The banging on the door gets louder and louder. Then there's an explosive crash as the door flies off its hinges. A tall man, maybe two-hundred-fifty pounds, dressed in all black with a scraggly black beard, powder-white face, and yellow eyes fills the doorway. He's holding a long-barreled pistol at his side.

Susan and Geier freeze. Then Geier smiles, slowly lights a match to his pipe, and sucks in three quick breaths to fire up the tobacco. His grin widens, and he exhales a plume of blue smoke toward the ceiling. Turning his gaze back to the intruder, he says, "Come in. We've been expecting you."

. . .

POSTSCRIPT: the inspiration for *The Last Appointment* came from personal experience as a writer. As I was putting the final touches on my third novel, *NOT SO DONE*, in February 2020 in which a terrorist launches a pandemic in the U.S., the real-life pandemic struck us. I made a few minor changes to the manuscript to acknowledge Covid-19 but otherwise left that story element as originally conceived pre-pandemic. And in the same novel, I wrote about an attack on the U.S. Capitol, which actually occurred six months after *NOT SO DONE* came out. I had to wonder when those two real-life events happened after I had written about them, *what if?*

ZOMBIE PHONE

I first saw it resting in a planter next to our table at Café Cucina. A black rectangle was camouflaged against the dark soil amid the thick stalks of a corn plant. I bent down to take a closer look. *Somebody dropped their phone,* I think. I pick it up and tap the power button.

The screen lights up—CALL IN PROGRESS. Huh? I didn't make a call, and this is not my phone.

Renata pushes her long auburn hair from her face and stares at me. "What's going on?" she says.

"What do you make of this?" I say, handing her the phone.

The waiter arrives and hands us menus. "Today's specials are—"

I cut him off. "Give us a few minutes." The waiter snorts, pivots, and leaves.

The faint scent of garlic and onions lingers in the air. The late summer sun is streaming through the large plate-glass window beside our table. Renata angles the phone away from the window to avoid the glare. She works for Homeland Security. Both a bomb specialist and an M.D., she's one of the smartest people I know. That she would give me a second look, much less a second date astounds me. I work at NIH here in D.C., fiddling with the genes of deadly viruses all day, a boring and very geeky job compared to hers.

Renata's expression changes. Her lips tighten and her eyes widen. She puts her index finger up to her lips to quiet me and then draws a finger across her throat. I get the message. *Shut up.* Her persona changes again. She straightens up in her chair and forces a smile. "I think I'm going to have the *Tilapia Florentine.* You?"

Figure it best to play along. "Call me boring, but spaghetti and meatballs are the true test of a great Italian restaurant. Do that right and all the other fancy, dancy Florentine stuff will be good too."

Renata fakes a laugh. "OK, now that that's settled. Listen, can you meet me tomorrow at 2:00 in West Potomac Park by the railing along the river, across from the Jefferson Memorial, and bring along that sample we discussed?" She nods her head emphatically up and down, my cue.

"Sure. I'll bring you the latest strain, but you know what we're doing could get me in a lot of trouble."

She doesn't miss a beat. "I know. Just make sure you're not followed the way I showed you. Hey, listen. It's Sunday. We don't have to rush back to work or anywhere else for that matter. I'm not hungry. Let's skip lunch and go back to my place and have some dessert. I'll give you a taste of something you'll never forget." She winks at me.

I feel my face redden. This is moving much faster than I

expected. I mean it's only the second date. We just had a warm, sweet kiss goodbye after the first date. Thoughts are swirling in my head. *The phone? Meeting in the park? Sex? What's going on here?* I silently raise my hands palms-up, miming my question.

Renata taps the red button on the mysterious phone, disconnecting the call. She removes the phone's battery and SIM card. Then she takes a silver Faraday bag from her purse, puts the phone and battery inside, and seals it. "We'll have a look at this back at the office. Maybe we can figure out who it belongs to." She studies the worried look on my face. "It's a Zombie Phone," she says.

"What? What's a Zombie Phone?"

"Somebody wanted to listen to our conversation. So they hid this phone in the planter. He or she set the ringer to silent and the phone to auto-answer. We sat down and our intruder called this phone, it answered silently, and he or she was listening. It's high-tech and low-tech at the same time. Pretty clever, eh?"

"That's some scary shit. What do you think they want?"

"Not sure. That's why I made up that stuff about meeting in the park tomorrow."

"I got that part. That's why I played along. Obviously I can't share my work with anybody. So we're not meeting in the park tomorrow?"

"Oh, but we are meeting in the park. I'll have the place totally surveilled and surrounded. If that's what this phone is about, we'll find out and nail the bastard," she says.

"I never suspected our second date would turn into a spy novel, but I did like that part about going back to your place."

"Oh, that was an act too. The other possibility is that my ex-husband put the phone there to spy on me. I'll nail him too." She pauses, noticing my face fall. "Oh, don't look so disappointed. Once we get to know each other a little better, I might invite you over for a little dessert." She smiles and tears apart one of the dinner rolls sitting in the basket at the edge of the table. Chewing, she says, "Now, let's order lunch."

I'm not sure how I feel about all this. I've definitely lost my appetite. But looking into Renata's beautiful brown eyes and taking in her self-confidence, my nerves start to settle. The waiter returns and takes our order.

She pats her lips with her cloth napkin and reaches out, taking my hand in hers. "You know there's one other possibility." She pauses and tilts her head. "Your boss might want to have a serious conversation with you tomorrow morning, and you might need a very good lawyer."

POSTSCRIPT: I never knew about Zombie Phones until I met Kevin Murphy, a cybersecurity expert and subsequently read his book, *Is My Cell Phone Bugged?* Thank you, Kevin.

WORD DRUNK

"**S**top! Stop filling my head with your crazy nonsense," Renata cries.

"Sorry, I'm addicted to breathing and your crazy ex, Brad, almost put an end to that. It's not nonsense. Look at this." Juan lowers his collar, revealing an eight-inch cut across his neck, still oozing. "What the hell do you call that?" He asks.

"OK. What did you do to provoke him?"

"Nice. The assumption is that it's my fault, right?"

"Well, I know you and I know him. So odds are…"

"Look, I bumped into him at the Grammar Bar. You know, the one on 63rd. I should've told him to buzz off right then and there, but a free drink is a free drink." Juan drops into the overstuffed easy chair in Renata's fifth-floor living room overlooking the park. He just stares out the picture window at the lightly falling snow. The aroma of coffee lingers in the air.

"And?" Renata says, raising her eyebrows.

"We had a few drinks and got into an argument about gerunds."

"Gerunds? What are you talking about?"

"Like when a verb is acting as a noun. Like *Reading is my favorite pastime. Reading* is a gerund there."

"So, so what? For this, he slashes your throat?"

"It started to get out of hand when he said 'How do you like *banging* my Renata? Is that a good gerund?'"

"Wow. That's why Brad's an ex."

"So naturally I get really pissed off because…" He pauses for a long five seconds. "Because I don't think bang*ing* is a gerund there."

Renata gives Juan a swift kick in his right shin. "That's what pissed you off?"

Juan clutches his shin. "Ouch, that really hurt. I was just kidding."

"Glad you could enjoy a joke at my expense." Renata folds her arms and purses her lips.

"No kidding now, I think *banging* really is a gerund in that sentence."

Renata spins and gives Juan a harder kick in his left shin. "How's 'my boyfriend deserves a *thrashing*' for a gerund?"

Juan clutches both shins. "I thought you found my sense of humor, or should I say *joking*, attractive?" he says with a grimace. "Guess not. Anyhow, because he insulted both of us, I grabbed him by the throat and wrestled him to the floor. I tell him, '*Strangling* you would be worth the consequences.' I'm squeezing hard. The bartender says, 'No fighting in the Grammar Bar.' I finally lost my nerve and let go."

"Christ, Juan, serving time is not what you want to do. Didn't have enough wasting away in that hellhole in Guadalajara?"

"You're getting this gerund thing pretty good."

"It's *well*. Pretty *well*," she says.

"I'm not sure about that. Anyway, your Brad pulls out a stiletto, flips open the blade, and does this." Juan points to his throat. "He says, 'Killing you may be more enjoyable and a better gerund than screwing Renata.' He was about to finish me off when two beefy guys grab him from behind. I was lucky. They were off-duty cops in the bar discussing the pluperfect when the fight broke out. If it weren't for their fast thinking, I'd be your ex too."

Renata lets out a deep breath and her expression softens. "Do us both a favor. Stay away from Brad and don't go near that bar anymore. I'd like to keep you in one piece. Mourning is not as much fun as loving."

"Or schtupping." Juan smiles.

Renata's warm hand gently touches Juan's neck. "Let me get something to put on that."

"Thanks. Who knew grammar could be so dangerous?" Juan says.

POSTSCRIPT: *Word Drunk* is dedicated to my late mother-in-law, Florence Sandler, who was a Ph.D. professor at Seton Hall University, wonderfully creative, and an insistent grammarian.

RENATA'S DREAM

Renata caresses her warm cup of coffee in both hands. Despite being inside her own kitchen, she can see her breath. "We should try again," she says.

Only two legs in worn jeans protrude from under the kitchen sink. Rick slides out from under and stares directly into Renata's dark brown eyes. "Try again? To fix the sink or the marriage?"

She laughs. "Maybe both. But you fix the sink and the heater first and then we'll talk about the marriage. I'm so cold I can't even feel my toes."

Rick smiles. "I'd be happy to warm you up."

"The sink and the heat first and then we'll talk."

Rick shimmies back under the sink. "I probably should have worked on the heater first. It's freakin' cold under here."

"You always did have bad timing."

"This damn old house . . . We should have sold it after you kicked me out. It's a money pit."

"And live where? With Aunt Thelma?"

"You don't have an Aunt Thelma."

"Right and that's why I had to stay here."

Rick wriggles out from under the sink again and wipes his hands on his pants. "Try the faucet now."

Renata pushes the faucet handle up, then left and right. "Seems OK."

Rick stands up. He's almost a head taller than Renata, but their eyes lock. Rick looks down at her cup of coffee. "That sure smells good. Can I have a cup?"

"I suppose, but then I have to get to work." She lifts a cup out of the cupboard and grabs the pot from the coffee maker.

"Another bomb threat?"

"No. This time it's a kidnapping, the son of one of my co-workers."

"So it's personal?"

"It's always personal. Now get your ass down to the basement and check out the oil burner." She slaps him on the butt.

"Hmm, I like that. Do it again."

"Maybe later, maybe never. It depends."

"Depends on what?"

"Depends on my day. Depends on whether I have heat when I get back home. Depends on whether I can ever trust you again."

"One slip and I'm sentenced for life. You are and always were the love of my life. Ever hear of second chances?"

The alarm clock chimes. Renata thrashes under the sheets and her eyes slowly open. They feel swollen, the lids stuck together. She rolls over and silences the clock. Rick's picture stares back at her. *What a fucking dream*, she thinks.

She stares at her pale face in the mirror and runs her fingers through her mussed hair. *I've got to get dressed. Funeral's today.* A newspaper clipping hangs from a corner of the mirror. A familiar face is in the picture next to another picture of a crumpled Jeep. The Headline reads:

"Connecticut Man Dies In Icy Crash"

Renata's eyes well up with warm tears. She wraps her arms tightly around herself. *If only I had given him that second chance. If only.*

Sometimes there are no second chances.

POSTSCRIPT: the character Renata appears in three of my novels and a few of the stories that follow. My editor asked about her several partners and former husband. All I can share without spoilers is that Renata enjoys life.

LOVERLY

The gravel driveway is long and winding up to the Riverdale Assisted Living Center in Scarsdale. Rich gets out of his Crown Vic and takes a minute to take in the puffy morning clouds doing their slow dance in the early fall sky. The scent of freshly cut grass lingers in the air. Life is short and bittersweet, he thinks. Scarsdale is one of the most affluent towns in America, not that it matters in this case. What matters is that it's close to where his sister Margaret lives, so she can check on Mom regularly. Rich feels pangs of guilt for visiting so infrequently but being assigned with DHS to California and then D.C. has made it harder.

Rich's mother, Alice, is in Stage 5 of her Alzheimer's journey. Her trip down this path is mostly pleasant but sometimes scary and confusing. She has good days and bad according to Samantha, her nurse. There is no earthly light at the end of this road. Hopefully, there is a divine one.

Rich checks in with Samantha. "How is she today?"

"Today is a good day. She may remember you. Why don't you see if she'll go outside? The morning is cool enough and the fresh air may do her some good."

Rich takes Samantha's hand. "Thanks for being so kind to her."

"It's not hard. She's a sweetheart."

"I miss the way she was, but I'm sure you hear that all the time."

"Getting older is about adapting, Alzheimer's or not."

"I understand. It's just a loss. That's all."

"Yes, and despite the series of losses we suffer from age, there is much left to appreciate and enjoy. Try focusing on that." Samantha gestures toward the hall. "She's in her room."

"I will," Rich says. Samantha pivots and saunters toward the reception desk. Rich can't help noticing the gentle sway of her hips.

He heads down the hall and knocks gently on the open door to Alice's room. His mother is in a rocking chair, attempting to knit something, which looks like a tangle of knots. She looks up. "Rich, you're home from school. How was your day?"

Rich forces a smile. "It was good, Mom. Would you like to go for a walk outside? It's an *extra-special day.*"

She smiles broadly. "You remembered I always taught my students that every day is an extra-special day." She turns back to her chaotic knitting.

He reaches over to lightly take her arm. She recoils. "Don't touch me. You took advantage of me once. Shame on me. You won't do it again."

Rich wonders what cruel memory she is reliving. "It's me,

Mom, Rich, your son. I saw that they are serving ice cream outside. Would you like some?"

Her demeanor instantly changes. "Ice cream. I love ice cream. Do you think they have chocolate sprinkles?"

"I bet they do. Come, let's go see."

She drops her knitting in a nearby garbage can. "Let's go. I want vanilla with chocolate sprinkles." She stands, but still slightly stooped, heads for the door.

Rich circles behind her as she heads out, retrieves the knitting, and puts it on her chair. He hears her from the hallway, "C'mon. What are you waiting for?"

He hurries into the hallway, gently guiding Alice downstairs and onto the expansive lawn. There is a Good Humor truck ringing its bell, last call. Rich buys two ice cream cones, one with sprinkles and hands it to his mother. They share a bench in a white Gazebo on the edge of the woods. A cardinal alights on the railing and chirps a few notes.

"Rich, what was that song we used to sing when we did the dinner dishes at night?"

"We sang lots of songs, Mom. Mostly show tunes."

And as if she is a blossom opening up to the sun and not failing at all, she launches into... "All I want is a room somewhere/ Far away from the cold night air/ With one enormous chair/ Oh, wouldn't it be loverly?"

Rich joins in. "Lots of chocolate for me to eat/ Lots of coal makin' lots of heat/ Warm face, warm hands, warm feet/ Oh, wouldn't it be loverly?..."

Then Alice stops abruptly and seems to shrink back into herself, like a tulip closing at the end of the day, "What did you say your name was?"

Rich's eyes water. "Rich, your son, Mom."

"Oh, Rich, yes. Did that bully pick on you again at school today?"

"Yes, Mom. He did."

"Remember, bullies are just weaklings in disguise, trying to make up for their small penises. You stand up to him. Show him who's the better man."

Rich blushes and smiles for real this time. "I'm trying every day, Mom."

"Good," she says as a tear runs down her cheek. "Because today is an extra-special day."

POSTSCRIPT: Loverly is taken from Chapter 43 of my third novel, NOT SO DONE. It stands on its own apart from the central story in the novel and seems to resonate with many readers. I wrote it from my personal experience with Alzheimer's, as my beloved and brilliant father-in-law succumbed to its deadly grip.

When my narrator, Daniel Greenberg, recorded the audio-book version of this chapter, I was brought to tears by his heartfelt, tender rendering of what I had written. When I praised him for his performance, he explained that his mother was currently in a nursing home with the same malady. His emotional rendering was imbued with his real-life sentiment.

DEATH BY DEVICE

Lea Swan parks her Audi just outside the yellow tape. Lights atop emergency vehicles are flashing. There's a crowd of reporters, and the smell of exhaust from the idling cars and trucks lingers in the air. Lea flips open her creds for the uniform guarding the perimeter, ducks under the tape, and wades through the cops and medics, moving toward her partner. Anwar Hamed is taking notes in an old-fashioned notepad, one leg up on the bumper of the ambulance.

"What've you got, partner?" Lea asks.

"Took you long enough to get here. What gives?" Anwar says.

"I had a hot date with Johnny Walker, but I'm here now. So spew."

Anwar smirks, closes his notebook, and turns to her. "You and Johnny need to take a little time out . . . Looks like another suicide. Chen is over there doing his ME schtick. No sign of foul play. The vic left a note on his computer. Pretty depressing."

"I don't get it, third one this week. Something's going on. This is not normal. Oh, and me and Johnny go way back. With a job like ours, Johnny and I won't be breaking up anytime soon. Let's go inside. I wanna see that note."

Gary staggers to the dining room table, sits, and fires up his laptop.

I apologize for the length of this note, but I couldn't sleep. I'll have plenty of time for that later. Besides, I'm a writer, and when writers can't sleep, they write. OK, seems like things were going well in my life and then suddenly it all turns to crap. Has that ever happened to you? In my case, it started with something simple—an everyday kind of thing really. I had this brand new Moonbeam Toaster, four slices. The right side two slices stopped working, couldn't get the toast to stay down, and the LED screen on the damn thing kept saying *Error*. Pissed me off. Toasters are about as simple as tech gets. I have my mother's old two-slice from forty years ago, works fine. So I take the dead thing out to my garage and throw it in the trash bin, curse, and slam the garbage can lid. I was feeling better already.

That's when the trouble really started. I returned to my kitchen where I began to make myself a midnight snack but had lost my appetite. So I pulled out my bottle of Jack and poured a shot. After gulping down a good belt, I turn to my hockey puck-sized digital assistant. Living alone, she some-times makes good company. The sound of another human voice, or maybe a human-like voice, usually calms me. "Lexis, what's the weather forecast for tomorrow?"

"I'm sorry. I cannot answer that question," Lexis said.

What? That's weird. I tried again. "Lexis, what's tomorrow's weather?"

She answered, "I'm sorry. There will be no weather tomorrow."

"Fuck you!" I said. I know, I know, it's just a machine.

"I'm sorry. I have not learned how to do that yet," she said.

Yikes. I was suddenly reminded of that great bit Woody Allen used to do about when all the appliances conspire against him. They even all get together in the living room to have a meeting about it. The memory makes me smile briefly. But what if this is more like HAL from *2001?* I need some sleep. It's already one AM. I throw back the last of my bourbon, feeling the sweet burn in my throat when the lights in the kitchen go out.

Ugh. "Lexis, turn on the lights," I shouted back toward the kitchen.

"I'm sorry. Something went wrong," Lexis said.

"I'll say. Dumb idea hooking up my lights to you in the first place." I fumbled around and grabbed a flashlight from the counter. At least that worked. Every other kitchen appliance has broken in the last month. Get this. My digital double-oven has all its electronics, control panel, and circuit board right above the ovens. Guess what? When the oven gets hot, it melts the components. Brilliant design. Then my four-burner stove, the premium flat-top design I paid extra for, only heats on high or is off. Nothing in between. Don't get me started. My fancy-dancy built-in combo microwave-exhaust-stove-light-fan no longer cooks anything, but the light, fan, and timer work. Yippee, two out of three. The company that made all these wonderful devices also makes jet engines. God help you if you fly in one of those planes. I'm sorry. I'm rambling. I'm tired and more than a little tipsy. My nerves are on edge. I'm in the dark, and it feels like my whole house is ganging up against me. Writing this all down like this helps.

OK, OK. I'll go outside, get away from this digital crap. Some cool night air might help, I thought.

I turned the door handle, but the deadbolts were locked. "Lexis, unlock the doors."

"I'm sorry. Something went wrong," she says again.

"Lexis, open the fucking door," I said.

"I'm sorry. I don't appreciate your tone," she said.

"What? Are you fucking kidding me?" I said.

"Would you like to hear a joke?" she says.

"You're a joke. A bad joke. Now let me out of here," I said.

"Here's a bad joke . . . " she said.

At this point, I don't even remember the joke I was so upset. On my back door, there are two panes of glass on the top half of the door. I have a key. I thought maybe I can unlock the door from the outside. To do that, I had to break the glass. So I rammed my fist through the pane nearest the door lock. Shit, the glass cut my wrist. By reflex, I pulled my hand back, and the glass cut deeper. Blood was running down my arm and dripping onto the floor. I still had the flashlight and navigated to the towel closet, grabbed a towel, and wrapped it tightly around my wrist. Should I go to the hospital, call 911? I thought. No, the bleeding seems to have stopped. I'll be OK.

Gary returns to the laptop in the dining room and drops into his chair.

I'm not sure what it is. I just know that writing helps me deal with the anxiety I've had all my life. I can only write it all out and usually, that makes me feel better, for a little while at least. So that's why I'm doing this now.

I mean, in general, I like technology. The Internet has made my life as a writer infinitely better. What would we do without Google? I can even edit my work on my smartphone on the run. But some things just shouldn't be digital, like ovens, refrigerators, and toasters. The old analog devices lasted much longer, less to break. They were even easier to operate. You didn't need any help from an eleven-year-old genius to figure them out. OK, I'm doing it again. I'm sorry. No, I'm not. Lexis is sorry. I'm just going to throw all those fucking devices out, starting with her. I can't take this anymore.

Uh, I feel a pain in my chest. Trouble breathing. Maybe I should call 91—

Swan and Hamed are in the dining room now. All the lights are on. Swan looks down at the body, still slumped in the chair, blood dripping from his right wrist onto the soaking towel on the floor. A crime scene photographer is flashing pictures. "Chen, cause of death?" Lea asks.

"Well, he bled out for sure. The cut wrist. He also has a pacemaker that may have malfunctioned. You know those things are connected to the Internet these days," Chen says.

"Yeah, I know. That's scary shit right there," Lea says.

"But I don't get it. Why would he break the glass in the

door? When the cops arrived, all the doors were unlocked," Anwar says.

"Look at the note he typed on his laptop, right here in front of him," Chen says.

Lea presses the power button, activating the laptop's screen. She reads,

I apologize to my family for the mess. I just can't take this anymore. Better to end it now. Cutting my wrist just seemed like the simplest way. I'm sorry.

Love, Gary

Lea scratches her head. "That's it. That's all he wrote?"

"That's all they found," Anwar says.

Chen lights up a Marlboro and exhales a plume of pungent, blue smoke. "Suicide," he says, starting to fill out the report on his clipboard.

"I want to check one thing. Gary has one of those digital assistant thingies." Lea returns to the kitchen. "Lexis, what's the last thing I asked you?"

"You said," Lexis says and then switches to a recording of Gary's voice. "Lexis, turn on the lights."

Lea just stares silently at the black hockey puck.

Anwar breaks the silence. "OK, what's that tell you? The lights are on."

Lea scratches her head again. "Yeah, but did you hear the tone in his voice. He sounds really stressed."

"Of course he's stressed. He's about to commit suicide. How else would he sound?"

"Yeah, I guess you're right," she says.

"You bet I'm right. Open and shut. Case closed, right?"

She sighs. "OK, case closed."

Anwar smiles. "You can go back to Johnny now. He's waiting for you."

POSTSCRIPT: I have always been enamored with gadgets. So it's no surprise that I would be an early adopter of smart speakers, aka voice assistants, when they first appeared. And then I wondered what happens when this technology with the help of artificial intelligence becomes more human and takes on a personality. And then what if...

ZOMBIE PHONE 2

It was a mild, sunny day. The early spring breeze caressed my face. The fragrance of the brilliantly blooming cherry blossoms hung in the air. Just as Renata and I planned, I was waiting by the railing across from the Jefferson Memorial. We agreed to meet there after our date yesterday, brunch at Café Cucina. The truly odd thing about that date was that I discovered a black cell phone hidden in a planter next to our table. Renata explained that it was a Zombie Phone, placed there to silently answer someone's incoming call, so they could listen to our conversation. *But who?*

Renata coaxed me to meet her again today, knowing we were being overheard. *Where is she?* I thought. I worked for the National Institute of Health, she for Homeland Security. Knowing that someone was listening, we pretended I was going to hand over to her a deadly virus sample or some other valuable, highly classified substance. Now you know as much as I knew, except Renata promised she'd have surveillance at the arranged meeting, and she'd catch whoever bugged the prior day's conversation. I checked my watch, 2:16. Still no Renata.

Leaning on the rail, I gazed at the reflection of the grand rotunda dedicated to Thomas Jefferson. *In God We Trust, everyone else pays cash.* Not sure what made me think of that. Maybe it was the creepy sting operation Renata somehow sucked me into. I didn't even really know her that well.

As I turned around to lean back against the railing, a tall, striking woman with wild red hair approached me flashing a wide smile. *Who is this?* She gave me a tight embrace and said, "Oh, I missed you so much, It's wonderful to see you again."

My arms, hesitant at first, seemed to have a mind of their own as they wrapped around her waist. Then she planted a long, lingering kiss on my willing lips. Her lavender perfume intoxicated me. And as quickly as this encounter started, it ended. She stepped back and said, "Gotta go now. I'll call you later." Just like that, she turned and left. I watched her confident stride as she receded into the distance, that red hair flying and waving in the wind.

Huh, what just happened? I wondered. Some innate reflex made me pat my back pocket to make sure my wallet was still there. It was. I rubbed my other pockets. To my surprise, in the right pocket of my coat, I felt a lump. Inside the pocket, there was something smooth and round that hadn't been there before. I hadn't put it there. *The woman, the redhead?* I wanted to look at the small cylinder, examine it, but not there in public. If there was surveillance, me extracting a vial from my pocket could blow the whole thing. Wait, maybe the redhead was setting me up, placing a vial of something dangerous, insidious, classified even, in my pocket and then—

I saw two men rushing toward me. They were both wearing black coats with dark sunglasses, a barely visible wire curled from their collars to their ears. The taller man said, "Would you come with us, please?" They each firmly grabbed one of my arms.

"That wasn't a question," the shorter man said, tugging me forward.

"Wait, what's going on? I didn't do anything," I protested.

Neither man responded. They forcefully led me to a waiting black Chevy Suburban and pushed me into the back seat. Out the dark-tinted window, I saw Renata emerge from behind one of the cherry trees. Her lips were moving. She seemed to be talking into her wristwatch. The Suburban gunned it, whipping my head back.

Looking at the back of the two men motionless in the front seat, I asked, "Where are we going?"

No answer. I was screwed.

We arrived at a five-story granite building on Martin Luther King Jr. Way. Another man and woman, also in dark suits, emerged from the building. The woman opened the car door and said, "This way, sir."

I didn't move. She seized my arm with a vise-grip and yanked me out. I tried to pull my arm free, but her powerful grasp didn't give. It was foolish to fight my way out of this Kafkaesque situation. I thought I'd be better off attempting to talk my way out. I've always been good at that. Since I was not a physically powerful child, I quickly learned that persuasion and humor were my superpowers. But these guys in the dark suits seemed in no mood for jokes.

They left me alone in a dimly lit, green-tiled room. The only furnishings were a metal table bolted to the floor and two metal chairs. The room smelled like Lysol. After waiting a minute alone, I turned the doorknob. Locked.

Breathe. I struggled to calm my racing heart. I sat. I paced. There were no windows and they had taken my watch, so I couldn't tell how much time had passed. It seemed like hours. I was thirsty. I needed to pee. Banging on the door brought no response. I pounded on the door until my hand hurt. Nothing.

I'd pee in the corner if I had to. I slumped down in one of the unforgiving steel chairs. Closing my eyes, I drifted off... I was back at the Jefferson Memorial, still impatiently waiting. A woman approached, but this time it was Renata. Her welcoming brown eyes and pouty smile moved something inside me.

"I'm so sorry to be late," she said. "We just needed to get everyone in place. We think we know who was listening on the Zombie Phone yesterday."

"Who?"

"Just kiss me and it will all become clear," she said.

I looked into her penetrating eyes. There was so much there I didn't understand but longed to know. I wrapped my arms around her and kissed her hard. An electric warmth seemed to come through her lips and fill my whole body. I have known other women, but never felt this way before, this intense.

Suddenly, a man burst from the trees running toward us. He had a gun and fired, one shot, two. We ducked to the ground. I put my body on top of Renata's, protecting her. More shots. I turned my head as the assailant crumpled to the ground like a rag doll. Three more men appeared from the woods, guns drawn. They approached the fallen, lifeless man. After kicking his gun away, they holstered their weapons and looked in our direction.

I slowly rose. Then I saw it. A red plume of blood on Renata's white blouse. I rolled her over and listened to her chest. She was still breathing. "Renata? Renata!" I cried.

Her eyes flickered open. "Did they get him?" She whispered.

"Yes, who was he?"

"My Ex. He was a dangerous man and a Russian spy," she muttered.

"Don't talk," I said and waved an arm at the three agents.

"I'll be OK." Renata's voice trailed off. Her eyes closed and her head lolled to the side.

A loud noise woke me from the dream. The door to the green-tiled room swung open. It was Renata. My heart skipped a beat. "Thank God, you're OK," I said.

She furrowed her brow and said, "I'm OK, but you're in big trouble." She studied me and shook her head. "I knew I should never have married you."

NIRVANA SODA

"Refresh your thirst and achieve enlightenment." – Nirvana
Soda

Nancy pulls a soda can from the cooler at Hook's Deli near Dumbo in Brooklyn.

"Just try it," Nancy says, handing the faux tie-dyed colored can to Michelle.

"No! What is it?"

"It's just a soda with a little extra."

Michelle rotates the cold, colorful, yet otherwise ordinary-looking twelve-ounce can.

She reads the front of the label out loud: "Enlightenment in a can! Refresh your thirst and you may see new worlds at the same time. Many have achieved a new level of consciousness. When imbibed regularly, your life could be extended, possibly forever."

"What a load of crap," she says.

Nancy laughs. "You're such a stiff sometimes."

Michelle turns the can over and continues reading: "Each Nirvana drink is infused with 99 mg of premium X22 isolate. Our isolate is made from all-natural, celestial products. We blend our isolate with natural flavors to create one tasty, transcendent beverage. Nirvana is made in a state-of-the-art, food-grade production facility with the utmost care for the safety and satisfaction of our customers."

"More bullshit! But wait, here it comes, the disclaimer. 'Although studies are underway, results so far are anecdotal. This product is relatively new—so life extension cannot be verified for several more years. Note: forever is a very long time.'"

"First thing that makes any sense." Michelle convulses with laughter.

She wipes a tear from her eye. "OK, how much is this wonder drink?"

"Dunno. Let's find out," Nancy says.

Cigar smoke wafts through the air of the landmark deli. Michelle looks down at the worn oak floors as they approach the counter. When she looks up at the cashier with the shaved-head and fish-hook earrings, the source of the cigar smoke becomes evident.

After studying Hook for a moment she raises the can and asks, "How much?"

Hook grins and chews on the cigar. "Only $9.95, but you can buy a case for a hundred bucks. Save $20.00."

"You're shittin' me," Michelle says. "Ten bucks for a lousy soda?"

"You're not just buying any old soda, my friend. You're

investing in a chance for enlightenment and a shot at immortality. That's a helluva bargain, don't you think?"

"He's got a point there," Nancy says.

Michelle snorts. "Even if I believed these crazy claims, what guarantee do I have that I'll transcend this life?"

"Hey lady, it's only a ten-buck soda and I said you'd have a chance. Look, I can't keep this stuff on the shelves. You see this," he says, pointing to the lottery machine. "I sell thousands of dollars' worth of tickets a day. Nirvana soda is just like that. Maybe it works and maybe it doesn't. But as they say, *you've got to be in it to win it.*"

They both giggle. "It's like a tax on the stupid," Michelle says.

"Which, the lottery or the soda?" Nancy asks.

"Look, girls. I've got payin' customers waitin'," Hook says, motioning them away.

As they move to the side, a tall, muscular man with tattoos festooning both arms drops a case of Nirvana soda on the counter and pulls a C-note out of his worn jeans. He slaps it on the counter. Hook punches a key on the antique register. It chimes and the drawer opens.

"Thanks, Joe. See you tomorrow?" Hook says.

"You can count on it," Joe says, lifting the case and grinning at Nancy and Michelle as he brushes past.

"Unbelievable," Michelle says.

"Joe swears by the stuff—one of my best customers. So whaddya say?" Hook says. "You get a good drink out of it. And maybe… well, you never know."

"Ain't that the truth," Nancy says. "You never know."

Michelle hesitates and then digs a ten-dollar bill from her

shorts. "OK, it's a hot day. I could use a drink. I'll pay my tax." Cold beads of sweat form on the can. She pops it open and takes a tentative sip, then a few more enthusiastic swigs. She offers it to Nancy. "Taste it."

Nancy raises her palm. "I'm already hooked on cigarettes and alcohol. I don't need to add to the list. It's all yours."

Hook displays a Cheshire cat smile. "How do you like it?"

Michelle smacks her lips. "Not bad. At least it's cold, but I don't feel any different."

"Give it some time."

"Like forever." Michelle snickers. "What if it doesn't work? Like no enlightenment, no transcendence, yadda, yadda?"

Hook cocks his head toward the lottery machine. "Then you buy another one."

"'Scuse me, folks." A man in black shorts, black t-shirt, and black ski mask pushes them aside. He's sipping a Nirvana soda, looks at the label and throws the half-full can at Hook, barely missing his head. Brandishing a .38, the man shouts, "Transcendence, my ass. Empty the register." He waves the pistol. "Now."

Michelle and Nancy slowly back away and then crouch behind the display of Ding Dongs. Hook hits a button on the register, which dings as the drawer slides open. The intruder reaches over for the cash. Michelle spots a fifteen-ounce can of Cento Crushed Tomatoes. She slowly rises, winds up, and throws a fastball striking the man between the shoulder blades. He's briefly stunned. Hook seizes the opportunity. He slips his left hand under the counter. In a flash, he fires both barrels of a 12-gauge shotgun into the robber's chest at point-blank range. The blast hurls the man against the Twinkies stanchion as if he were a rag doll, knocking over the display and spilling its contents onto the floor.

A deafening silence fills the air, along with smoke and the smell of cordite. Nobody moves. Blood oozes out onto the floor from the man's still-warm body. Michelle and Nancy rise tentatively from their hiding place.

Hook drops the shotgun from his trembling hand. "Are you ladies OK?"

"I think so." Michelle is breathing heavily. "Are you?"

"Yeah, I'm OK." Hook blows out a long, slow breath. "Like I said, you never know."

Nancy looks down at the motionless corpse. "The soda didn't work for him, I guess."

"Then again, maybe it did," Michelle says and takes another sip.

POSTSCRIPT: I wrote this story after visiting my local deli. At the cash register, I noticed an extensive display of CBD-infused products including cans of CBD Soda. Cost? Five dollars per can.

THE SCIENCE OF REGRET

The early morning light filters through the blinds in Juan and Renata's third-floor Park Slope Brooklyn apartment. Juan rolls over in bed and kisses Renata on the back of her shoulder. "I need some coffee badly," he says.

"Tough night? I didn't even hear you come in."

"Sorry I was so late."

"Studying?" Renata asks.

"Sorta. Exams next week. Took a break and stumbled on an article about Pluribus, a program created by Carnegie Mellon and Facebook. This sucker beat five top poker pros at no-limit hold 'em."

Renata turns around to face him, her long brown hair spread across her pillow. "Fascinating..." she says as she suppresses a yawn.

Undeterred, Juan continues. "Remember when IBM's Big Blue beat Gary Kasparov, the world chess champion, twenty years ago? That was a big deal...proved that a computer could be programmed to beat the best human at something."

"How did it do that?" Renata perks up.

"From what I know, it learns and can calculate millions of possible moves several steps ahead to plot the optimal next play. The best human player can only figure maybe eight moves ahead."

"OK, the computer is a better, faster calculator than a human. So what?"

Juan sighs, exasperated... "It's not just a 'stupid computer trick.' A couple of years ago, Google's AlphaGo program beats the Korean world champion at GO, an even more complex and subtle game."

"OK, genius. Get dressed and we'll make your emergency coffee run. Do I need to call an ambulance or can we just walk there?"

Juan laughs and throws a pillow at her. "Smartass."

They leave their apartment and walk a block to Cafe Grumpy on 7th. The aroma of coffee wafts through the air while Bob Dylan's, "Don't Think Twice" is playing in the background. A line of people waits to get to the counter, all noses pointing down to glowing cell phone screens.

Juan taps his foot and fidgets. "Maybe if making coffee could be done by computer, I'd get my fix before midnight."

"Calm down, hombre. Hey, let's finish the computer game discussion... About the poker program, sounds like more numbers and more calculations to me. The computer can see the entire board in chess and GO, then calculates the moves from there, right?" Renata says.

Juan's eyes light up. "Yeah, that's true, and that's why the

Pluribus program beating hold 'em is such a big deal." He waits for a response, but Renata is taking in her surroundings, the exposed brick walls, the driftwood tables, millennials on one side, and the retiree coffee klatch on the other.

She turns back to Juan. "Go on."

"With hold 'em, the computer and the players can't see all the cards until the last card is exposed. Imagine trying to play chess if you could only see half the other player's pieces. How would you do?"

"I'd get crushed."

"Exactly! That's why most poker players are losing players. It's a game of incomplete information. The players take the information they do know, like the cards in their hands, calculate their odds, and bet or bluff accordingly. That's also why there's no bluffing in chess or GO."

"Can't you feign a bluff in chess or GO, making it look like you're doing one thing when your real plan is a zinger that your opponent doesn't see? I don't get it. Why no bluffing?"

"It's not that easy. As you said, in chess and GO you can see all the pieces. You can't pretend or bluff that you have a better position than is readily apparent on the board. But in hold 'em, you can't see my cards or the cards to come on the flop. So I can pretend or bluff like I have a big hand, make a large bet, and maybe get you to fold a better hand. All because of incomplete information."

"Kinda like life, huh? We make decisions all the time without knowing all the facts."

"Yep, we take risks. We try to figure the odds of the best outcome, but it's still a gamble."

"Like our relationship?"

"Um, I hope not. I mean I'm *all in* on this relationship, but there are no guarantees, are there?"

"Nope. We don't know the future, but we're both taking a gamble."

"And enjoying the game. Don't forget that part."

"OK. So how does this Pluribus beat the pros with incomplete information? Maybe we can learn something."

"Like the chess and GO programs, it learns. But it does something else called *Counterfactual Regret Minimization*."

"What the hell is that?"

"It learns from every hand, especially the ones it loses. It says like, 'OK, I fucked up that hand. What can I do better next time?' And it does it over and over again, thousands, even millions of times until it perfects a better strategy than the pros."

"Something like learning from your own mistakes..."

"Right and with the power of a computer, it can crunch a lifetime of learning into a few days."

"Reminds me of something our friend Sam says. 'I hope I live long enough to benefit from all my mistakes.'"

"Ain't that the truth."

They reach the counter. Renata orders her favorite cinnamon dolce creme and Juan orders a large iced coffee with an extra shot.

"So why are you thinking about this regret minimization stuff now?" Renata asks.

The redheaded barista rings up their order. "That'll be $8.32," she says, looking at Juan.

Juan shuffles his feet and turns to Renata, his head bowed.

"Because I lost all my money at poker last night. Mistakes were made. Can you pay?"

Renata's face flushes. She inserts her Visa debit card into the reader. "Now I understand the regret part." She snickers. "I'm practicing some Counterfactual Regret Minimization myself right now."

POSTSCRIPT: Robotic computer programs, called *Bots*, are currently mimicking human players online. Using Pluribus-type algorithms, these bots are beating unsuspecting amateurs who play poker for real money in online card rooms.

THE END OF THE LONG RUN

"Bad beat, again," I said and Neil raked the pot. It was Tuesday night at our weekly poker game. My wife, Monica, and Neil and his wife, Gloria, had had a regular bridge game for years. When we decided to be more sociable, adding Steve and his wife, Marge, we had to switch games. As an avid poker player, I suggested Texas hold 'em where anywhere from two to twenty-three people can play on a single deck of cards. They agreed and seemed eager to learn the game. They became pretty good at it too.

After I lost the third pot in a row, I remembered a saying from Amarillo Slim, the famous Texas road gambler, and I said, "'It's not about results… it's about decisions.' If I make good decisions, I'll win in the long run. You'll see."

Neil laughed and said, "How long is the long run?" He stacked his newly-acquired chips in nice, neat colorful towers. "Really, how long is that? I'd like to know."

"We never really know, do we?" Gloria said.

"Yes, but we make assumptions, don't we? Otherwise, why save for retirement or have a rainy day fund?" Monica asked.

"I'll buy in for another fifty dollars," I said, handing a crisp Ulysses S. Grant to Monica. Since she was so good with money, we all trusted her to be the banker.

This wasn't anything like the higher stakes I'd play at a casino or at the World Series of Poker. Still, as Nick the Greek famously said when caught playing a dollar-two-dollar game in his old age, "Action is action." Playing for any kind of money tends to focus the mind and bring out the competitive spirit. At least, it does that for me.

Yet, whoever won on a particular night didn't matter much. We all enjoyed playing regularly in Steve's basement, which he'd remodeled as a game room. In addition to his well-stocked bar, the game room featured an official green felt Texas hold 'em table in the shape of a stretched oval. Since Steve was a serious smoker, he allowed and even encouraged smoking in his man cave. As a non-smoker, I put up with it, but would immediately throw my smoky clothes in the hamper as soon as I returned home from the games.

Steve dealt out the next hand. "I'm sorry Marge couldn't make it. Bad cold. She didn't want to pass it around. Cards and chips are the next best thing to bodily fluids for passing germs."

"Well, I hope she gets better soon. Tell her we miss her… and her money." I looked down at the two cards I was dealt—king of hearts and king of spades, second best-starting hand in poker. I bet five dollars. Neil called the bet. Gloria, Monica, and Steve folded.

Gloria lit a cigarette and headed for the bar. "Neil, would you like a drink?"

"Yeah sure, get me a beer." Neil looked at me and snickered. "You and me, again."

Steve then dealt the flop, the first three of five community cards that we shared to make our best five-card hand. King-deuce-deuce. A full-house for me, almost a perfect flop. It was so strong I didn't want to lose Neil by betting. I rapped my fist on the felt, a check-no-bet gesture, passing the decision to Neil. "Twenty-bucks," he said, sliding a stack of twenty white chips into the pot.

Hmm, what could he have? I rechecked my cards, two kings were still there. I scanned Neil's blank face for tells. Nothing. Gloria handed Neil the beer and he took a big gulp.

Neil smacked his lips and said, "C'mon, Sam. Time for one of your great decisions."

I hesitated, then shoved my chips into the middle, "All-in," I said.

Without a moment's hesitation, Neil said, "Call," and counted out fifty in chips to match my all-in.

"Flip 'em over. Let's see," Monica said.

I turned over my kings. "Full-house, kings over deuces."

Neil paused and silently showed his king of clubs and deuce of diamonds. He had a full house, but a lesser one.

"Deuces over kings," Steve said. "Still two cards to come. No more betting. Sam's all-in."

Steve dealt a harmless fourth card, the queen of clubs. Then it was time for the river, the final card. There was only one card out of thirty-eight left in the deck that could beat me. Steve and I both stood up, hovering over the table. Steve flipped the last card, a deuce of spades. "Quad deuces. Neil wins," Steve said.

"Shit, shit, *shit*," I blurted. I was stunned, but I knew poker. This happened. It was just like in life. Everything's going along swimmingly. Then, bam! Something totally unlikely, a black swan, a one-outer on the river, comes along and felts you.

"The long-run must be a really long time, " Neil said, wrapping both arms around the pile of chips, pulling them in like they were his children.

Then the vibe in the room suddenly changed. I felt a chill. It wasn't clear what triggered her outburst at that moment in front of us all, but Gloria's face turned red and she said to Neil, "Talking about decisions and bodily fluids, I know about you and Marge. I can't believe that after nineteen years you would do this to me, to us, to the kids."

Neil stopped cold and stared at Gloria. He started to cough, choking on his own spit, "I'm... I'm sorry," he muttered. His face turned as gray as his hair, and he fell face-down into the stacks of chips.

"Call 911!" I shouted. Rushing to Neil, I pulled him from the chair to the floor and rolled him onto his back. Chips showered around us. I put my ear to his nose. Nothing, but I could smell the whiskey on his breath. Leaning over Neil, I started chest compressions. 1... 2... 3... Stop, hold his nose. Breathe into his mouth. Nothing. Repeat... over and over. After ten minutes, I fell back onto my butt and shook my head.

The EMTs rushed in. After checking for a pulse, they unraveled their AED paddles and, "Clear." Again, "Clear."

Nothing. Again, nothing. They looked up at us. Nobody spoke or moved. Gloria slumped stone-faced back in her chair. The EMTs put Neil on a gurney and rolled him toward the door. "We'll take him to Baxter Memorial just in case. Meet us there."

Now that's a bad beat, I thought but didn't say it.

"Now what?" Steve asked into the air.

Gloria, as if in a trance, tapped a pack of cigarettes against her hand, pulled one out, and lit up. She blew a stream of blue-gray smoke toward the ceiling and said, "Deal."

POSTSCRIPT: The idea in my story of poker players continuing a game after a player drops dead is inspired by World Champion Doyle Brunson's true story in his *My 50 Most Memorable Hands*. In Hand #10, Doyle and the others were playing four days and nights straight when Virgil, who had been drinking and smoking heavily, keeled over and died at the table. Once he was taken away, the game resumed for another 24 hours.

REALITY CHECK

"I had a weird dream last night. Like I wasn't alive, but I wasn't dead either. Just spinning and falling and numbers fading in and out everywhere." That's how I started off the conversation. The day was sunny, and ribbons of light danced lazily through our kitchen window. "In the dream, there was a clock too, an old grandfather clock. Strangely, the hands were racing backward."

"Sounds scary. Are you OK?" Monica felt my forehead.

"It got me thinking. Sounds scary, but I keep asking myself, what if we're not real?"

"Sam, what are you talking about? We've been married ten years and honestly, sometimes I wonder how we made it this long." Monica smiled and pinched my cheek.

The coffeemaker beeped and I poured a cup, offering it to Monica. "Want some?"

"Is it *real* coffee?" She put it to her nose. "Smells like real coffee." She sipped. "Tastes like real coffee. Well, at least we know the coffee is real."

"Seriously, I've been thinking about this. What if we're just an idea or a dream, somebody else's dream? Or maybe we're just characters in somebody else's story? How would we know?"

"OK. I'll play along, but it sounds like you've been channeling Borges again. I just did a taste and smell test with the coffee. The fact that I can experience those things keeps me from being a character in a novel... doesn't it?"

"Maybe, but then again, maybe not. In a novel, characters smell and taste things all the time. They feel pain. They love. They die. That doesn't make them real."

"What about our eight-year-old son sleeping in the other room. Are you telling me he's not real? As a mother, I can tell you that giving birth to him was really real."

"Maybe you thought it was real, like telling a story. The story has a certain life of its own. If it's told well, full of tastes and smells, sounds and sights, it can certainly feel real, but it doesn't have to be. Take what's going on in the world today. We're inundated with lies that we are told are real. You may know they're lies, but many people believe them. For them, reality is different, it's changed."

"I see what you mean. Reality can be a slippery thing sometimes." She snickered. "Reality isn't real, huh?"

"Exactly. It's a conundrum, a paradox," I said as I spooned some more sugar into my coffee.

Monica, who is a psychologist, brought up Google on her phone. "Did you ever hear of Cotard's Delusion? It's a mental illness listed in the DSM where the subject believes that all or part of them doesn't exist. Maybe that's what you've got."

"It was just a question, granted a big question. I'm not crazy. I don't feel depressed or anything like that. Just out of curiosity, how do doctors treat this Cotard's?"

Monica tapped a few more keys. "Drugs or electroconvulsive therapy. Maybe you should see someone."

"So I guess that means Descartes, Plato, and Aristotle were all mentally ill." I snort. "Don't call in the white coats just yet. Let's get back to the question. Is there a test or some way you can prove you are real and not a character in the mind or dreams of an author? I'm a science guy. I'd like proof."

Monica put down her coffee, wrapped her arms around me, and gave me a long hot kiss. "How's that for proof?"

"I have to say Dr. Sunborn, that I approve of your methods. I'm just not sure your proof is conclusive."

"Evan is still asleep. If you care to step into the bedroom, I'll show you some conclusive proof."

"I accept the challenge." We climbed the stairs to the bedroom where reality disappeared for at least an hour.

Monica was lying close to me, her head on my chest. I felt a warm glow from the touch of her skin. "That certainly felt real to me..." I stared up at the ceiling. "...But it isn't proof. It could have all just been made up, a very sexy love scene in a story."

Monica pushed me away. "If that wasn't real, you do need help."

"No, no, it was great. Come back." I pulled her back in close again.

She didn't resist. "I'm not sure what to do with you."

"You seemed pretty sure a few minutes ago."

She punched me in the arm. "You know what I mean."

I stifled a laugh. "You know how Descartes' proof was his statement, *I think, therefore I am?*"

"Yeah, I know it. But putting on my psychologist's hat again, I always thought Descartes' argument was pretty weak. I mean how do we know he was thinking anything. Too subjective to be proof."

"For once, we agree." I turned and looked Monica in the eyes. "I think I have it. Are you ready?"

"OK Einstein, what is it?"

"*I wrote this, therefore I am.*"

POSTSCRIPT: Enough said.

PART II

MEMORIES & DREAMS

A BELATED PRICELESS GIFT

I never knew him. He died when I was a year old. But I heard growing up that my father, when he was alive, liked to take home movies. I had never seen any of these movies, but I inherited his Kodak movie camera, a 16-millimeter in a thick leather, protective case.

Two days ago, early morning I received an email from my older brother. "You're not going to believe this. Login to my Walgreens account. Here's the password. Use my email as the username." OK, I think. I've got a day full of meetings starting at 7:30 AM. My new novel just came out this week, and I have a list a mile-long of things to do. I'll check this out later. The day blows by. Another email from my brother. "Why haven't I heard from you?"

This is unusual. I love my brother, but if we talk once a month, that's a lot. Why the insistence? Later, I think. I'm making dinner tonight. I cook. My wife and I eat. I zone out in front of Netflix. Time for bed. Check the phone. A voicemail from my brother. *"Did you get what I sent?"* I'm dead tired, but I better check this out. And then it happens—I enter a parallel universe.

Flickering to life in front of me is a little boy, a toddler in blue velour pants and zip jacket. The film frame jumps and jiggles. The color is faded Kodachrome. The toddler is walking toward the camera. Zoom out and an older boy is holding his hand. Cut to summer. There are flowers along a walkway. An older girl, maybe fourteen. The toddler is blowing on a red harmonica. Cut to fall. The toddler, now in a rust velour jumpsuit is raking leaves. The camera pans the front of the red brick house I was born in. Cut to winter. The frame jumps like there's no vertical hold. The toddler is now in a dark blue snowsuit, holding his brother's hand, still walking toward the camera. Snow is on the ground. The film frames sputter and it's over. The toddler is me, six decades ago. The cameraman with shaky hands is my father.

I'm stunned. Was that me? Did we dig up a time capsule

that I didn't know was there? And what about what's not on the film? The subtext, the backstory. The happy family, the cameraman. All that was about to change. The loving father, who doted on his young son, dies suddenly two weeks after that last winter scene he filmed. A heart attack at age forty-nine. The happy family is shattered. My vivacious mother is now sullen, depressed, and forced to work. She has three young children and can no longer afford that brick-front house, my parent's dream home.

Of course, I was too young to remember any of this. The details all came to me second hand from my late mother, and that young boy and the young girl, my brother and sister, in the film. I never knew my father, but I knew the *lack* of a father growing up. No ball games or father-son events for me, but look at all he missed. That generous, sweet man. So once I recovered from the surreal moment of seeing the two-minute film for the first time, I watched it many more times. I thought how lucky I am to have received this belated gift from my father, the cameraman, sixty-five years after its making.

And maybe, just maybe I can see back the other way through that movie camera lens, and my father will be on the other side, not so gone.

MISSING THE GHOST IN THE PALACE THEATER

A True Story –

My sister stumbled upon a fifty-five-year-old set of documents. Buried beneath the legalese, the text evokes a flood of personal memories as it reveals the story of a family in the 1950s. The sales agreement, mortgage releases, and title insurance papers on their face codify the sale of the Palace Theater, located in Orange, New Jersey, dated November 1953. The buyers were the Kridel family, represented by Myron and Jerome. The sellers were my family, the Levins, represented by my deceased father's brothers, Harry, Lewis, and Abe.

This is where it gets personal. From age seven on, I could walk or take the bus to the Palace on Saturday mornings. With my free passes to watch Sinbad, Godzilla, and Disney films, it didn't matter what was showing—I just went. My reading skills were a bit limited at the time, but I did understand the sign that said *Air Conditioned*. That was a big attraction too.

In the 1950s, very few places were air-conditioned, and movie theaters were among the first places where people could escape the summer heat. In fact, my failure at age eight to read the marquee led me alone to one Saturday showing of a very adult, tragically emotional film, *Imitation of Life,* with Lana Turner and Sandra Dee. This wasn't Sinbad—I cried my eyes out.

About those free passes. I had no real idea of how we got them. I knew my family had owned movie theaters at one time but no longer owned the Palace. When my sister gave me the contract mentioned earlier, it piqued my curiosity. I felt like Sherlock with a mystery and a hot lead to follow. My investigation started with my grandfather, Simon, who emigrated from Russia in the early 1880s at age fourteen. His parents sent him to the U.S. to escape the pogroms and the inevitable conscription into the Russian Army. His only possession was a large, very sharp pair of tailor's shears. He plied his trade as a tailor into growing a department store, which he later sold to Bamberger's.

Apparently, Simon was quite the savvy businessman. He bought real estate in Newark and the Oranges early in the post World War I boom when values were rising. When the depression crippled the country, the one thing people would buy, other than food, was an escape from the horrors of every day, and tickets to the movies were a salve for the pain. The Palace was built in 1918 and Simon acquired it in the 30s. Unfortunately, his five sons, including my father, did not generally have such fortuitous timing, the exception being the Palace Theater. They sold it for $210,000 in 1953, the equivalent of two million dollars today. With sympathy and knowing my father had died shortly before the sale of the theater, the Kridels gave my mother the free movie passes.

In retrospect, I believe it was all those Saturdays at the movies that sparked my imagination and kindled a love for storytelling. And maybe years later led to my becoming a writer. OK, what is the story hidden in the contract? One clue is *Schedule A* attached to the agreement of the "List of personal property located at the Palace Theater." Perhaps the most valuable item on that list was the "6 Carrier Air Conditioning Units—68 tons." The A/C in July was probably a bigger draw than the latest Elizabeth Taylor or Cary Grant film on the screen. Then there are the "1400 Theatre Chairs." So we know this was a big theater, probably three to five times larger than the average theater today. How about the "Stage Draperies" or the "350 Marquee Letters?" What picture does that paint?

The history of the theater gets more compelling when you learn that half the theater was in Orange and the other half was in East Orange. Back then, East Orange had Blue Laws, which meant businesses within the town could not be open on Sundays. On Sundays then, the left side of the theater was roped off and patrons were only allowed to sit on the right side in the town of Orange.

Then there's the 1942 picture above with the long line of people in front of the theater. The crowd was the result of a promotion—free admission in exchange for scrap metal to support the war effort.

The real story for me was that my father died at age forty-nine of a sudden heart attack. I was only a year old and I never really knew him. I heard from my siblings that he was a loving, generous man with a passion for making home movies. At the same time, due to my father's faulty will, my mother was forced to go to work full-time during the day to support her three young children. At night, she endured lonely evenings since the light of her life, my father, had been so unexpectantly snuffed out. It was a struggle for her both financially and emotionally. As a result, there was little time left over from her grinding existence for mothering. Hence the movies became, for me, a kind of cosmic connection to my lost father and an escape from a fractured childhood.

Sometimes now I have a vision, maybe it's more of a dream. I'm sitting alone in an aisle seat at the Palace Theater, buttery popcorn in hand. Laurel and Hardy are on the screen tripping over Christmas trees. It's Sunday and there is joyous laughter coming from someone, someone long-gone, on the right side of the theater.

MOON LANDING MEMORIES

I included the Moon Landing question in a recent newsletter to my readers and asked them to share their experiences. I was so delighted by their personal and intimate recollections that I asked their permission to share their poignant short stories here. Thankfully, most obliged.

#1 Adolescent Adventures

I'll start with my moon landing memory. I was 17 and had effectively run away from home for a week. I was staying in a guesthouse in Provincetown on Cape Cod, watching on an old black-and-white TV with the other guests (which is a whole other story). We all seemed to relish the rapture of that transcendent moment. Two weeks later I drove my 1968 GTO to Woodstock. It was quite a summer. – Charlie

#2 Oscilloscope

I was working in a government R&D lab. We jury-rigged a receiver to an o-scope and watched the landing in living green. – George

#3 The Burbs

On July 20, 1969, I was two weeks shy of my 19th birthday and living in one of those little burbs (Cheektowaga) outside of Buffalo, NY. I was working for a small ad printing company that worked out of a basement under his home. At the time of Neil Armstrong's walk, we were all upstairs standing around the boss's TV set watching the moon landing (and, yes, we had to clock out if we wanted to watch). I remember the boss, a German immigrant, saying something along the lines of "I can't believe he actually did that!" We were all mesmerized. – Becki

#4 – I Was 5

I was 5, and Dad said watch the TV because this is something never seen before. I'm surprised I remember it. – Julie

#5 Dusty Stuff

July 1969 I was working at Butlins Bognor Regis (a holiday camp on the south coast of England). I'd made friends with some Americans who were staying there. We sat up all night with beer and snacks watching the landing as you can imagine it turned into quite a party! The amazing thing is I still remember it vividly all these years later. I've found over the years that if you ask anyone what Armstrong first said they reply "One small step for man one giant leap for mankind,"

What he actually said was "It's some kind of dusty stuff I can stir it around with my foot". I prefer this one. It's more honest, but I suppose he had to go with the official blurb. – Barrie

#6 Staying Up Late

Yes, I was around for the lunar landing. I had turned 5 at the beginning of July. I remember mom and dad more or less making my brother and I watch. They felt this was an important point in history, which of course it was. We all watched in Dad's den in the basement. We didn't have AC so it was much cooler in the basement. I was allowed to stay up late so it was really a big deal! – Cathy

#7 – 5-Inch Screen

1969 seems so long ago, although when it comes right down to it, it's not so long. Below is a photo of our daughter Brenda Gelean watching the moon landing on a 5″ TV screen with us in our bed on that spectacular night in 1969. On the other hand, maybe 1969 is farther back than I think, since even Brenda's kids are all in their teens now. Three of our grandchildren. All four of our grandchildren arrived after the year 2000.

Watching the landing in the middle of the night in North Vancouver, BC on a 5″ screen, tiny TV set with our youngest baby about 6 mo. old. Seems like she enjoyed it. – Betty

#8 Rabbit Ears

On 7-20-1969, I was 19-years-old and watched the "moon landing" with my kid brother and new husband of two months. Since we were poor college students, we were lucky to have owned a 10″ black-and-white tabletop TV with foil on the "rabbit ears" antenna for better reception. I can still see us huddled together with our noses only a couple of feet from the screen of the TV in our very small apartment "dining room." It is really strange how "50 years" sounds so long ago, but it doesn't really feel all that long ago. – Leigh

#9 The Rental

Well, here's my little story. My wife's birthday is on July 20. When the moon landing took place, I was in the Army (lucky me!), but we didn't have a TV. That's because I was so well paid (LOL). Anyway, we both wanted to watch the landing, so we rented a small TV for a month so that we could. And yes, we got ourselves up at 3:00 AM or thereabouts to watch. My wife was 75 yesterday, and yes, we have a TV now—we're planning to watch a Mars landing when it takes place—and yes, it WILL take place, hopefully in our lifetimes. - Frank

#10 En Swisse

I was in a small hotel in Switzerland. A group of guests and house staff clustered around a small B&W television set in the lobby. No one said a word for the duration of the moonwalk. I was a foreigner watching a fellow American on REALLY foreign soil. But there was something that transcended our geopolitical differences. It was a great moment for everyone on the planet. - Steve

#11 Nuts?

The summer of 1969 I was a new college grad with my first job as a reporter at a suburban Chicago newspaper. I rented a room in an Evanston apartment of a Northwestern University Ph.D. student in Astrophysics, or something in that genre. In anticipation of the moon landing, he rented several TVs in order to be able to simultaneously watch every channel's coverage of the event. (Was that three TVs, or four? At any rate, far fewer than he'd need today.) That seemed nuts, although even then I had a guarded admiration for anyone who takes their interest in a subject into extreme territories.

As it turned out, this fellow was extreme in his interest but definitely not nuts. He went onto a long career with NASA and remains a respected journalist and commentator on space exploration. I've not spoken with that roommate since. That summer was a dividing line for a lot of us, including me. - Bob

#12 4-Inch TV

For the landing, I was back in North Carolina visiting family. For the launch, I was working in the computer data communications center at Goddard Space Flight Center. I had a 4″ square slow scan TV unit fed by a camera on top of the vehicle assembly building, giving me as close a view as possible of the launch.

For the landing, I woke up my niece who was about 6, to watch the astronauts step out onto the lunar surface at about 3:30 the following morning. - Malcolm

#13 Humphrey

My parents found out about the moon landing in the oddest way. In July, 1969, they were on vacation in Russia. Needless to say, there was a blackout on news about any Moon Shot. However, during a tour of the Kremlin, they met Hubert Humphrey, who was meeting Russian officials. It was Hubert Humphrey who told my parents about the moon landing. – Jonathan

#14 Popcorn

I remember that my whole family with mom and dad were all in the living room watching the tv as the astronauts landed. It was amazing to watch it with the whole family and a few friends that didn't have a tv came over to watch it with us. We were all waiting we had popcorn and koolaid to celebrate the moment with everyone. It's all we talked about at home and at school for at least a week. I'll never forget it! - Evelyn

STOP THE WORLD MOMENTS

So I'm at a critical point writing the climax to my latest thriller, *STILL NOT DEAD,* and I need to solve this puzzle: what event can I create that would stop almost everybody in the world from doing whatever they're doing for at least a second? Sounds crazy, right? Well, our heroes need a distraction, a diversion while they execute a delicate maneuver that will impact every living being on earth for .3416 seconds.

Writers, especially crazy sci-fi-thriller writers like me, have to solve storyline problems like my split-second diversion quandary all the time. So how do we do that? For me, I searched my personal memories for moments in my life where the world literally stopped.

Certainly, there have been epic global events in all our lives, events where everyone dropped what they were doing and glued themselves to a TV, and before that, a radio, and now a phone or a computer. Some of these events were grand

and wonderful, like the first men landing on the moon in 1969. Everybody, and I mean everybody, was watching and listening. I wrote about this in my post, *Moon Landing Memories*, and over twenty readers added their own recollections of, *where were you that day?* But unfortunately, more of those memorable stop-the-world moments seem to have been tragic, like 9/11.

If I had to pick the one event in my life that stopped everything around the world, it would be the Kennedy Assassination in 1963. Some of you may not have even been born yet. I was twelve years old. That day, that freeze-frame in time may have encapsulated everyone's typical day gone awry.

Where was I on 11/22/63? Let me set the stage. My father died when I was a year old. My mother, who was a typical 50s housemaker was thrown into a strange reality the day my father, only forty-nine years old, collapsed on the bathroom floor. A heart attack. The love of my mother's life, the father of three small children, and the breadwinner was suddenly gone.

Her financial situation forced her to go to work, which meant from age six, I was pretty much on my own most of the time. Now, one of my biggest shortcomings back then was that I had buck teeth, a defect that subjected me to the endless scorn and ridicule of your typical schoolyard bullies. I can still hear, "Hey, Bugs Bunny!"

To address this deficiency, my mother signed me up with a young orthodontist in Irvington, New Jersey, several miles from our home. When I say he was young, I'm guessing I was his first patient out of dental school and accordingly, he cut my cash-strapped mother a break. Since my mother was busy all day, every day at work, I would take the bus alone from East Orange to Irvington every few weeks to have metal and rubber bands added, removed, and added again for nine years (I know, it's a really long time, maybe a record). From age eight to sixteen, I dutifully made the pilgrimage to Dr. Dawdle's office to be stretched, fitted, plucked, and pulled (the doctor's name has been changed to protect me from a lawsuit and to reflect his alacrity).

When I say I took the bus, it was a bit more involved. I would walk the two blocks from our apartment on South Harrison Street down Elmwood Avenue to the bus stop on Sanford Avenue and wait twenty minutes to a half-hour for the #24 to Irvington. After a twenty-minute ride left me off at Springfield Avenue, I would then walk another mile to the doc's office. On the walk, I would cross a bridge over the Garden State Parkway, a six-lane Indy 500 that people think of when they think of New Jersey.

It was crossing the bridge that taught me the meaning of the word *vertigo* in a very visceral way. I had to force myself not to look down for fear of plunging headfirst into the insane traffic. Combine that with the car exhaust fumes, in the days before catalytic converters scrubbed the noxious car emissions, and I felt like this whole routine was punishment for some unspoken crime. Me, a twelve-year-old Kafka in a cross between *The Trial* and *Groundhog Day*. Anyway, the entire trip took me about an hour and a half each way. A three-hour commute for a 30-minute session in the torture chamber.

Now you have the context. So on a fateful day, November 22, 1963, I was on my way back home from the orthodontist, waiting for the bus on the corner of Sanford and Springfield.

There was a late fall chill in the air. It was sunny and people were going about their business. Suddenly a woman with a long red coat and swirly black hat ran into the street, stopping traffic. She shouted the words I'll never forget. "The president's been shot! The president's been shot!"

The world stopped. The cars stopped. People crowded around the appliance store window staring in shock and disbelief at the black-and-white images of the Parkland Memorial Hospital waiting for news. Men wept openly. Strangers hugged. Then it started, almost with a whisper, "O beautiful for spacious skies..." Others joined in until everyone in full voice sang, "God shed his grace on thee..." When it was over, there was an eerie moment of utter silence. Then quiet nods, handshakes, pats on the back as people drifted off back to their no longer normal lives. And there I stood on the corner of Sanford and Springfield. Not yet a teenager, growing up that day.

Similar scenes took place not just in the U.S. but around the world. Walter Cronkite, with tears in his eyes, recited what little he knew at the time about what actually happened. The gunman on the sixth floor of the Texas School Depository Building. Maybe another on the grassy knoll. The black limousine, the president, and Jackie, and Governor Connelly. The secret service agent climbing on the trunk of the car, all in vain.

Yes, the world stopped that day and for several days after as we learned about Lee Harvey Oswald, and then two days later Oswald was shot by Jack Ruby. All very weird and mysterious, the stuff that bore conspiracy theories for decades to come.

Back to my writer's quandary. I needed an event like the Kennedy assassination that would stop everything. I think I found one and you'll have to read *Still Not Dead* when it's published this year to find out what happens. But I can tell you this much: after nine years of regular visits to the orthodontist and six years after President Kennedy died, it was time for me to head off to college. On my last ever appointment (I could drive to his office by now), Dr. Dawdle fitted me for a retainer designed to lock my top and bottom teeth into place all night, every night for the foreseeable. Great. When I left his office for the last time, I made a decision. It wasn't a tough decision, and I made it quickly. On Springfield Ave, I found the nearest garbage can and dropped my new, unused retainer into it. I had more important things to do.

LOVE IN THE PARK

A few months ago, I was looking for a book on the lonely bookshelves in our living room when I stumbled upon a box I had not seen in forty-eight years. Could it be? Opening the box, there rested an eight-inch reel of Super 8 film, the long-lost, original and only copy of *Love in the Park*. A flood of warm memories and emotions washed over me. This was a movie, the final project we made for a film course in my senior year at the University of Rochester.

In 1972, you did not make movies digitally or on video. You shot them in 8mm or 16mm or the latest format, Super 8. There were no VHS or DVD movies to buy or rent, but you could buy full-length films on Super 8 from the Blackhawk paper catalog. Being a lifelong movie fan, I did just that. I still have my Super 8 projector and a movie collection that includes Charlie Chaplin shorts, Buster Keaton, Laurel and Hardy, and the full-length original *Phantom of the*

Opera with Lon Chaney Sr. They were all silent films and my wife, Amy, and I would throw parties for friends, playing the old movies accompanied by music from my vinyl collection. For Halloween parties, we showed *Phantom* accompanied by dulcet and spooky organ music.

Love in the Park was my joyous attempt to honor those old treasures and create a modern-day silent short. We shot the film on a deep winter's day in Genesee Park and surrounding environs. This was much more than a home movie. We recruited actors, including Amy, and shot hours of film. I was particularly proud of the tracking shot we filmed of the characters running, my camera-in-hand hanging out the passenger side window of my GTO while my co-producer, Steve Meyrich, drove.

After the film shoot was complete, it took several days for me to make cuts and edit the movie down to eight minutes. For those edits, I hand-spliced the film and used tape to hold the pieces together. After opening the lost box this summer and realizing what I'd found, my second thought was, *is it still watchable?* Yet, I was too afraid to run it through my old projector, fearing the tape holding the film together would be too brittle and break.

So began my search for a company that would convert my half-century-old film to digital while handling it with kid gloves. I finally found a well-reviewed company, Legacybox in Tennessee, and shipped the reel off, fingers-crossed that they could save it. Two months later it was done.

Love in the Park is naturally a love story, boy-meets-girl. They fall in love, break up, and reconcile in the end. You've seen it a million times. The difference in our story is that the lovers' emotions, passion, impatience, anger, and excitement are mimicked expressively by a pair of S*hadows*. Maybe it's because my new wife (still happily married forty-nine years later) played the female lead, or that my friends so enthusiastically volunteered to play a part, or that it captures a young, beautiful creative time in our lives. Maybe it's the sweet-sour experience of first loves. Take your pick.

Albeit the film faded a bit and was darker than I remembered, and the original music was gone, it was still an untold thrill to see that movie again. Over the years I lost touch with those players, but I did track down my co-director, Steve Meyrich, and one of the *Shadows*, Jon Gottlieb. For them, like me, it was a gift of an unexpected, yet joyful blast from the past.

I'm not sure what anyone today would think of our amateur effort on that arcane medium, but have a look and let me know what you think. I've added music and uploaded the 8-minute movie to YouTube-- just search on "Love in the Park 1972." Maybe it resonates and will bring back some memories for you too.

CLOUDY WITH A CHANCE OF IGUANAS

D id you catch the story last month from the National Weather Service ("NWS") in Florida predicting that iguanas may start falling from trees? It can be dangerous—they grow up to five feet long and weigh up to twenty pounds. Might be a problem if one lands on your head!

The NWS tweeted:

"Jan 21—This isn't something we usually forecast but don't be surprised if you see Iguanas falling from the trees tonight as lows drop into the 30s and 40s. Brrrr! #flwx #miami"

NWS Miami @NWSMiami · Jan 21, 2020
Jan 21 - This isn't something we usually forecast, but don't be surprised if you see **Iguanas** falling from the trees tonight as lows drop into the 30s and 40s. Brrrr! #flwx #miami

Tuesday, January 21, 2020

Falling Iguanas Possible Tonight

South Florida Low Temps Tonight:

You can Google the full NWS coverage of the forecast, but that's not why I'm writing this story. Although it's bizarre and funny, which appeals to me, the unexpected forecast brought back memories of my decade-long relationship with an iguana, one that's inextricably intertwined with the early years of my marriage. If that doesn't pique your curiosity, I don't know what will. Read on.

It started when I married my high school sweetheart, Amy, after maintaining a long-distance relationship with her through college. Year one, we rented a three-bedroom apartment with a kitchen, dining room, living room, and an enclosed porch on the second floor of a two-family house in Rochester, New York. The rent was a staggering $160 per month! The apartment was a dream come true, a block from the lovely Cobbs Hill Park where we played tennis and took in local softball games on warm summer evenings. I can still smell the lilacs there for which Rochester is known.

Since Amy was supporting us as a teacher while I was

finishing my last year of school, majoring in philosophy and Ancient Greek—imagine the job prospects. The low rent was a blessing. In our new home, we had no furniture, save for a single twin-bed mattress that I'd "borrowed" from college. Amy slept on the mattress and I slept on the floor. This got old quickly, and Amy sent me on a mission to buy a mattress. Her only requirement was that it be a Posturepedic. While she was at school teaching, I visited the local Sears. Never having shopped for or purchased a mattress before, I had no idea what I was doing nor did I really understand Amy's brand requirement. So I purchased a Sears-O-Pedic mattress, a great improvement for me, but a major disappointment for Amy. I mean it had "O-Pedic" in the name so what's the difference? This was the first of many trial-and-big-error learning experiences on my way to becoming a better husband. Fortunately, Amy stuck with me and learned to love the mattress—or at least pretended to.

Anyway, where does the iguana come in? Bear with me, I'm getting there. On our first anniversary and in appreciation of our unlikely love story, Amy bought me a gift. No, it wasn't a "proper" mattress—it was a six-inch-long, bright green iguana. Huh? Well, it made perfectly good sense—she knew I was allergic to animal fur and thought I'd appreciate the unexpected quirkiness of it. She was right, as always. As a lifelong movie buff, I named our new pet Caligari after the bizarre 1920 film, *The Cabinet of Doctor Caligari*. It's a classic and the name seemed to befit this odd creature.

At first, we let Caligari have free range of our apartment. His favorite hangout was on the trunk of a corn plant we'd purchased to liven up our scantily furnished home. The trunk of the plant was maybe two inches wide. Caligari would dig his sharp claws into the softwood and hang. Since Caligari's body was wider than the plant's trunk, it was a constant source of amusement when we moved about the living room and Caligari would rotate his body around the trunk to hide from us. His assumption must have been that if he couldn't see us, we couldn't see him. Sounds like some politicians we know.

The free-range approach to iguana-rearing was OK for a while. We even had friends leave their iguana, named Tennessee, with us when they were on vacation. Caligari and Tennessee got along fine in their own way. You see iguanas are cold-blooded animals like snakes. They didn't show much affection and the word "interpersonal" is not in their vocabulary. It was more like what Amy and her teacher colleagues would call *parallel play*.

The free-range experiment ended when Caligari went AWOL. We frantically searched the house and finally found him comfortably resting in our oven's broiler, enjoying the warmth of the gas oven's pilot light. We were relieved we hadn't cooked him by accident. To prevent future potential tragedies, I bought an aquarium replete with stones and branches to hang on. Caligari's new home measured one-foot by two-feet. Most important, a 60-watt light bulb heated it— Iguanas need warmth to survive. That's why Caligari gravitated to the cozy broiler. And that's why iguanas fall from trees when the temperature falls below fifty degrees—they literally freeze up and can't hold on to the trunk.

After two years in Rochester, we rented a U-Haul and moved to Boston where I had been barely accepted to law school—a whole other story. On the trip from Rochester to Watertown, Massachusetts, where we were lucky to find the bottom floor of a house at a reasonable rate, Caligari made a daring escape from this cage during a pit stop. Not wanting to miss the action, he perched himself on my left shoulder—you should have seen the gas station attendant's face when I rolled down the window!

Now, one thing we didn't know about iguanas is that they not only grow, they *really* grow. In Boston, Caligari outgrew his first cage and I bought a larger one. Two years later, we moved to the Hudson Valley of New York and needed a bigger aquarium still. A few years after that, we bought our first little house in the woods by a stream in New Jersey. By this time, Caligari had grown to four feet long. I built him a four-foot by eight-foot cage out of plywood with a glass front and big branches to hang on. This was like a luxury iguana condo that came with perks, all the lettuce and mealy worms he could eat.

The food seemed to agree with him because he continued to grow. Caligari's ever-increasing size became a problem. Do we give him his own room? This little house only had two bedrooms and Amy was expecting our first real child. So no, our house was just too small for him. Reluctantly, we put a classified ad in the local newspaper (this is pre-Internet, pre-Craigslist) to try and locate someone who would give our beloved lizard a loving home. A week later, Ted, and his ten-year-old son, Jimmy, showed up. Putting your pet of ten years up for adoption can be an emotionally fraught endeavor. We thoroughly interrogated Caligari's would-be new parents. Apparently, Jimmy had several snakes and other reptiles. He understood their food and habitat needs. It seemed like a good fit. We wistfully bid Caligari goodbye.

You'll be happy to know that we received a call some years later from Caligari's adopting father, Ted, to inform us that Caligari was doing just fine and yes, he had grown but had free range of their warm basement. We were pleased for our dear pet. His new life certainly beats falling from trees.

TRIBUTE TO THE UNSUNG HERO WITH A THOUSAND SMILES

"You better come right away," Ann urged. "I just got a call from Harry's daughter. He's leaving us. I'm on my way to his house right now."

Harry, my unsung hero, was dying.

"We'll be there as fast as we can," I assured her. Harry's girlfriend of ten years, Ann, was not one to push the panic button, so I knew Harry's demise must be imminent.

This time I didn't hesitate about jumping in the car when the call came. I say *this time* because of a similar call I received forty years ago when my young sister-in-law was killed by a drunk driver. My weeping father-in-law placed the call, and my reply was "*Should we come home?*" Dumb. But when you're young, death is something foreign and far away, something that happens to someone else. I had not yet learned to speak its language. Now I am unfortunately all too fluent.

I fully expected that by the time Amy, my wife, and I arrived at Harry's house, he'd be gone. This time was different, extraordinary. To my surprise, Harry's daughter and a couple of other relatives we had never met greeted us with hugs. It certainly didn't feel like Death was in the house yet.

Harry's family had arranged for a hospital bed to be moved into Harry's room and for hospice people to make regular visits. Ann was sitting quietly by Harry's side, holding his hand. Harry's eyes were closed, but he was breathing. What struck me the most was his angelic, almost magical smile. It was otherworldly, like maybe he was simultaneously here and someplace else, his face a celestial window into worlds we only dream about. I will never forget that smile as long as I live.

As Amy and I talked and reminisced, Harry reacted with even bigger smiles, only interrupted by occasional winces of pain. His eyes remained closed through it all. Harry had been blind for years, so it really didn't matter.

So how did a white man—back then a kid—become close friends forty-five years ago with a black man, thirty years his senior and from such different backgrounds?

I met Harry when I was a college student working summers in my soon-to-be-wife's family business, which was owned and run by my father-in-law. All I knew then was that Harry ran the warehouse and I handled the inventory. A couple of years after graduating and a brief stint at law school in Boston, I returned to work full-time in that family business, which I eventually ran. Harry and I, in a way, became co-conspirators, getting things done in new ways that sometimes rankled other family members. His unflagging work ethic and ever-upbeat attitude inspired everyone around him. He even graciously agreed to mentor two of my nephews during the summers and vicissitudes of their adolescence. His lessons in hard work and discipline seemed to stick. They never forgot him.

Eventually, the family business was sold, and age caught up with Harry. Cancer, glaucoma, then blindness took its toll, but he never lost that smile. It was in his later years as I faced middle age, that Harry became a real inspiration in my life as I watched members of my own family not handle aging well, full of crankiness and constant complaints. What did they have to complain about compared to Harry? He was abandoned by his family as a child, never completed high school, served in the army, swept floors for a living, had a son who was murdered in Germany, lost a granddaughter to lupus, survived three bouts of cancer, and lost his sight. Yet he always had that "Harry" smile. Despite his disabilities, he got up and out every day, went to church and, although blind, took art classes. He created sculptures and collages, sometimes winning awards for his work.

Harry and I kept up by phone and occasional visits. I would pick him up and drive him to family events, the most somber being the funeral of Lewis Sandler, my beloved father-in-law mentioned earlier. Lewis saw something special in Harry. After hiring him for maintenance work, Lewis realized how smart and driven Harry was. Plus Harry seemed to have an innate sense of how to connect with others in a meaningful way. Despite the racism that was pervasive in the 50s and 60s, Lewis promoted Harry above his white colleagues to warehouse manager. Every time I saw him in his later years, Harry would tell the stories of how my in-laws saved his life. I never really grew tired of these stories because I knew how much they meant to both of us.

As unlucky as Harry was in many aspects of his life, his outlook and perseverance brought him a degree of good fortune. Ten years ago, he fell in love with a woman thirty years his junior. They met in church, and she stood by him until his last day. It certainly wasn't for the money because he didn't have much besides his social security. When Ann and Harry met that first time and fell into deep conversation, she revealed to him that she was white. His response was, "What difference does it make to me? I'm blind."

Harry's daughter gave Harry a place to live and cared for him when he most needed it. She told us, "We could have let him pass in the hospital, but it just didn't seem right. We wanted him home."

I feel blessed and lucky to have known Harry and learned so much from him. I learned about aging with dignity and being a role model of energy, perseverance, and outlook that could inspire younger people. I learned there is no place in a life well-lived for self-pity and grumbling. For that, I will always be grateful.

Amy and I left Harry alive and smiling two days ago, wondering how long he would last. The suspense ended today when I was halfway through writing this life story about Harry—not intending it to be an obituary. Ann called, choking back tears. "Harry passed away this morning." I'm sure he did so with grace, dignity, and above all, his trademark smile.

HEAVEN+

[Note: this short story thriller asks the question: *What happens when you subscribe to one-too-many TV streaming services?*]

How many streaming subscriptions do you have? Me, I've always been a film and television fanatic. I think it goes back to my childhood. My father and his brothers owned movie theaters, which meant from age two on, it was every Saturday morning at the movies. Free, hot, fragrant popcorn in a manilla brown envelope. Why it wasn't in a regular popcorn container is a story for another time.

Unfortunately, my father died young, forty-nine of a heart attack, found dead on the black-and-white-tiled bathroom floor. Every moment in time has a ripple effect. The big ripple for my mother, other than losing the love of her life, was being forced to go to work to support three young children. She made the best of it, but it meant the ripple for me was spending most of my childhood home alone. Just me and TV.

I can still smell the faint burning odor of the hot cathode ray tube that made televisions three feet deep in those days.

Just like parents fret now about their kids spending too much time on their iPhones, back then parents worried about their kids spending too much time in front of their RCA Victors. I knew the TV Guide schedule by heart. As a very young watcher, it was *Howdy Doody* and *Captain Kangaroo*. Harmless merry little kids' shows followed by the *Mickey Mouse Club*. Even pre-pubescent me, I knew there was something special about Annette Funicello, especially in a bathing suit.

A few years later westerns like *Gunsmoke, Wanted Dead or Alive* with Steve McQueen, *Rawhide*, Roy Rogers, and *Bonanza* were my daily bread. Oh, *Bonanza*! Lorne and Hoss were like family. On Sunday nights, Mom would watch Bonanza with me. After a hard week, but before the Cartwrights could save the ranch yet again from cattle rustlers, she'd fall asleep in her easy chair, a lit Marlboro dangling from her fingers. Then there was *Superman* in black & white, George Reeves leaping buildings in a single bound. Too bad he offed himself in real life at age forty-five. Too much Kryptonite I guess.

There were all those great comedies too like *I Love Lucy, The Jack Benny Show, Our Miss Brooks*, and *Abbot and Costello* where, with the two of them standing in front of the stage curtain, I heard *Who's On First?* for the first time. (Gratified to know that bit got them into the Baseball Hall of Fame), And there were comedies you'll never see again, and with good reason, like *Amos and Andy*. Who could forget Ed Sullivan who introduced me to Buddy Hackett and Don

Rickles and the Beatles? I'll forever remember that night in 1964, "I Wanna Hold Your Hand," and the screaming frenzied fans.

And maybe the show that still sticks with me, *The Twilight Zone.* Rod Serling and his adventures of *Eye of the Beholder* and *Nightmare at 20,000 Feet* took me somewhere I never imagined. He inspired me and I'm sure countless other writers for decades to come.

As a teenager, I was still glued to the screen. Now there was *Star Trek* and even Soap Operas like *Dark Shadows.* At this point, I had a television in my bedroom, uh-oh. So late at night was always Johnny Carson. A reliable smile and laugh as I drifted off to sleep with the end of the TV day flag still flickering on the screen. Yes, in those days TV was not 24/7. In the New York metro area, there were only 2-4-5-7-9-11 and 13 compared to the hundreds of channels now. They would sign off at midnight or one or two in the morning with a flag waving or a weird mandala-like graphic.

Anyway, here I am now, all grown up, twenty-five years of *Law & Order* later. Now it's Netflix and all the others, my broadcast TV with its endless commercials fading into the sunset. I stick with them for *Blue Bloods*, *The Rookie*, *The Resident*, all the *Chicago* shows—*Med, Fire, and P.D.,* but I can see the writing on the wall. It's just a matter of time. Millennials, including both my kids, don't own televisions. They stream it all. Broadcast TV will disappear when Betty White and Tom Selleck take their final curtain.

With all that history and me consuming stories like potato chips, this is right now the Golden Age of TV Drama. With streaming services, even some of my mid-life great ones have come back like *ER, St. Elsewhere,* and *The West Wing.*

So yes, I subscribe to Netflix, Hulu, and Amazon Prime, but I've resisted all the Pluses—Disney+, AMC+ (although I really would like to see *Law & Order U.K.*), and Paramount+. All those old networks and the new ones have a Plus. Isn't it enough already? How much can we watch? Stop!

Except... there was this pandemic. All bets on reasonably restrained TV time were off. Don't get me wrong, I have had a wonderful real life, what the kids now call IRL, I have a wonderful marriage. In fact, as I write this, it's my wife Amy's and my forty-ninth anniversary. We have two exceptional grown sons. I coached both their teams growing up and never missed any of their off-tune holiday concert renditions of *Jingle Bells.*

So I can imagine that one day, I'll be scrolling through my Xfinity dashboard, past Netflix and Hulu (Comcast adds links to the most popular pluses to keep me from cutting the chord) and there will appear a new service, *Heaven+.* I click. A two-week free trial. OK, fine by me. I agree to the Terms of Service (which I never read, do you?).

But what's playing on Heaven+? I click the guide. That funky end-of-day graphic appears. Wait, it's not just the end of today. It's the end of....

THE PERMISSION SLIP

While cleaning out my crazily cluttered attic filled with thirty-eight years of things my wife, Amy, and I don't need, but couldn't part with--broken chairs, boxes full of clothes, ancient computers, 80s vintage suitcases, and the like, I stumbled across something quite special.

Let me back up. If you're a procrastinator like me, there are only two reasons for cleaning the attic—because you're putting your house up for sale or you've come to grips with the fact that all those cardboard boxes sweltering at over one hundred degrees during the broiling hot summer are a fire hazard (our neighbor's house burned to the ground following the spontaneous combustion of Christmas tree decorations stored in their attic). But I wasn't selling the house. And although I had the nagging feeling the boxes were a fire hazard, it wasn't enough to motivate us to take action.

So what other reason could there be? Two words. Flying squirrels. Yes, there are such critters and a family of twenty really liked our attic. The old mattress—downright cozy. The insulation and blankets—absolutely divine. And the floor and every one of our possessions on it—the perfect commode. On Internet advice (not always reliable), I threw mothballs up there to drive the critters away. Well, that didn't work and had the added side effect of stinking up the second floor of my house. After more than a dozen visits from a rodent specialist, we learned that our involuntary pets were sliding through louver vents to go in and out. He put mesh over the vent and invited our friends to leave.

If you've never seen a flying squirrel, they don't actually fly. However, they do have extra skin flaps under their arms that let them glide from nearby trees to welcoming attics. They're kind of cute. Still, not in my attic, please. Once they departed and the attic was secure from invaders, for health and sanitary reasons, it had to be decontaminated. Notice I used a third-person pronoun there. I'm handy and do a lot around the house, but the thought of dealing with poop-laden artifacts from our past was a no-go.

To my relief, I discovered that there is a whole industry for attic specialists devoted to cleaning and sanitizing attics. Hooray—not cheap, but worth every penny. After some further research and negotiations, five brave men in hazmat suits and breathing devices spent eight hours removing everything from the attic, removing all the insulation, power-vacuuming, disinfecting, and replacing the insulation. It is now pristine, clean, and empty.

So what happened to all the accumulated stuff up there? Other than a couple of dining room chairs we forgot we had and a bag of old letters, our attic superheroes carted it all away, never to be seen again. A great feeling. Now for the best part. Amy started going through that old bag of letters we rescued from destruction and she found...

WARNER, JENNINGS, MANDEL & LONGSTRETH
Members New York Stock Exchange
744 BROAD STREET   NEWARK 2, NEW JERSEY
MArket 3-6480

What started as cleanup and remediation turned into a personal archeological or anthropological project. There were letters from long-lost friends, passionate love letters we wrote each other when we were in high school, and one particularly meaningful note for me--a permission slip.

The permission slip you see pictured above is from my mother written on my behalf:

"To whom it may concern,
My son Charles Levin has my permission to play 'Pocket
Billiards'
Very truly yours
Mrs. Yvonne B. Levin
377 So. Harrison St.,
East Orange, N.J
OR6-5432"

The pool hall I wanted to frequent required customers to be at least sixteen to play, and I was just fourteen. The note, the permission slip, seems straightforward enough but examined more closely, it contains clues to my mother's life story, a snapshot of the 1960s, and a hint of my relationship with my mother.

First, there's the actual content of the note. For her to write this note, I had to have asked her to let her youngest son hang around, unsupervised, at a seedy, smoke-filled pool hall. Why would she agree to that? I'd like to think it was because she trusted me, but that could only be part of the reason. I think the other part was that she was tired, worn out after losing two husbands who died young, the first at twenty-nine and the second, my father, at forty-nine, and working full time to raise three kids. My sister is thirteen years older and my brother is nine years older than I am. So by the time she got to me, it was pretty much anything goes. A current expression may capture it best. With this note, I think she was saying, "Whatever…(sigh)."

Now look more closely and notice the penmanship. My mother explained to me that she was taught Palmer Penmanship in school. She, like every one of her generation, learned to move their entire forearm when they wrote to create a flowing, smooth style. Her handwriting was always perfect, whereas my scrawl looks like hieroglyphs gone bad. Now everyone types with their thumbs. Nobody writes that beautifully anymore.

How about that phone number, "OR6-5432?" Yes, back then, everyone shared their phone numbers with the first two letters of the town they lived in. "OR" was for "Orange." When I called Amy to ask for a date (there was no such thing as texting then), I would dial on a rotary dial, SO2-3791. She lived in South Orange. My mother also took pride in the fact that she talked ATT into giving her such an easy, sequential number to remember. When she couldn't stand that I spent hours on the phone (remember this is high school), she got a second line. Liberation, I had my own princess phone in my bedroom with the number OR6-5431.

Finally, at the bottom of the note: "Warner, Jennings, Mandel & Longstreth," a stock brokerage firm. She worked there as the first female stockbroker ever in New Jersey. After my father died, his loss forced my mother to go to work to support the family. At first, she didn't know what she would do. She hadn't worked in years, not since she was a floor manager at Bamberger's in Newark. In the 50s, men worked and women stayed home with the kids, and she had three young ones. Suddenly at age forty with the death of my father, her world turned upside down. As unlikely as it seems, when she was a teenager she used to hang out at the local stock brokerage office, watching the ticker tape or the stock prices being posted and erased, posted and erased in chalk on a big blackboard. Being a numbers person, she just loved it. That was what she always wanted to be when she grew up, but there were no women stockbrokers. With a little encouragement from a friend, she studied, took her exams, passed, and got a job with a room full of men in Newark, New Jersey. Soon she was the top producer in the office. She could sell, really sell. She was rightfully proud of her new career.

Warner, Jennings, and its successors were bought out several times by larger and larger firms until my mother landed at the fifth successor, Thompson, McKinnon, where they promoted her to vice president. In 1984 at age seventy-two, she had her best career year. She was a force of nature. Unfortunately the following year Prudential bought out Thompson and on account of her age, they made Mom retire. It was the end for her. Husbands gone, kids gone, and the job that filled her days with challenging joy gone.

Then one awful day in 1989, I got a call from my sister. "I can't reach, Mom." We both rushed to her apartment in East Orange. The super had to break the door open. Mom had taken an overdose of pills. The sight of her barely breathing, prone on the floor with the empty bottle of pills beside her, haunts me to this day. She lasted two days in the hospital, and then she left us.

Before Mom died, I carried this note, the permission slip, around in my wallet for many years. Partly for its sentimental value and at age thirty or so (I had a baby-face back then), maybe I'd need my mother's permission for something. She passed away thirty-two years ago in June. At the time, she was only a few years older than I am now. Still, I think I'll put the note back in my wallet—the date is blank, so it should be good anytime. 'Cause you never know when you might need a permission slip.

THE LAST MINUTE AND A HALF

"If you knew you had a minute and a half to live, what would you do?"

This question struck me this morning while I was completing the New York Times Mini Crossword that I do first thing every morning. It took me one minute and thirty-two seconds. I enjoy doing the crossword. It's like brief mental calisthenics—it wakes up my brain and gets me thinking about words, which is probably a good thing for a writer to do. Before eating Frosted Flakes for breakfast, I eat words.

The Mini is also a good test of how awake and sharp I am that particular day. If it takes five minutes to solve, I probably should go back to sleep. My fastest time ever was twenty-nine seconds. If I wasn't so slow typing, I'd do better, but who am I competing against? Anything under a minute boosts my confidence in my illusory and fickle superpowers. Occasionally I can't solve the puzzle at all. In which case I'm just depressed for hours. Sounds silly I agree, but hey, to be a writer is to be a bit *off,* if you know what I mean.

Anyway, back to the bigger question—*if you knew you had a minute and a half to live, what would you do?* For me, it wouldn't be the Mini Crossword. Typical responses might be: kiss your loved ones goodbye, relive your life, pray for forgiveness for all your sins—aka the people you disappointed or screwed over in your life, or perhaps, just alert Mom and Dad that you'll be seeing them soon.

But why am I even contemplating the question now? Am I obsessed with death? If you've read my *NOT SO DEAD Trilogy,* you figured out that I probably am. Yet isn't death the biggest, high-stakes question of our life? For me, it raises other questions like, *why is life so short? Why do we have to die at all—what purpose does it serve?* I'm not alone in asking these questions. There are many entrepreneurs and scientists investing time and billions of dollars in finding a cure for death. You heard me, a *cure.* What? Yeah, they call themselves longevity entrepreneurs and longevity engineers. Their sole focus is to figure out how not to die or at least live five to ten times longer than we do now. Some of the big companies involved are Google, Amazon, and Facebook. For better or worse, the founders of these companies believe they can fix or solve anything. Being masters of the universe, maybe they can. Hubris, possibly, but worth a shot, right? Or is it? What would living forever be like?

Perhaps the other reason I raise these questions now is that with the pandemic, death is constantly in the news and is much, much closer than Afghanistan. It's prematurely striking down a friend, a family member, or a neighbor, even the president. Or for me personally, it might be because I had cancer surgery last year. Whatever the reason, one might call the above *pressing* questions. But I digress.

So it's your last minute and a half, the time it takes to do a Mini Crossword or get your coffee at Dunkin Donuts. I haven't figured out for sure what I would do yet. I don't think we'll really understand until the moment is upon us. It may largely depend on how you got to that last minute and a half. If it's as the result of a tragic accident or a sudden heart attack, you may not get that minute and a half at all. Not to be negative, but some people may be in great pain at the end and just want it to stop. All reasons to work on the question now. And hopefully, you will have that minute and a half to leave this world gracefully with your wits about you.

When my time comes, I hope to be surrounded by the ones I love, my wife, my sons, my grandkids (may there be many more), and perchance one or two good friends if I have any left. I'm sure I will tell them how much I love them all and say, "Thank you." What will it feel like? What will it smell like? If I had a choice, I'd pick the sensation of swimming in a cool lake at sunrise for one and the aroma of bacon cooking or coffee brewing for the other. How about you? After I've said my goodbyes, I'd expect a transition, a kind of meditative trance that will connect me with the divine. I may even see myself walking through the door into the light.

And then what? Do we join a sea of souls awaiting the

next incarnation, rise to heaven or go the opposite direction, or is it just lights out? Your guess and your faith are as good as mine. Of one thing I am certain: whatever happens, I know I will see you there. >>>

PART III

ESSAYS

A CURE FOR DEATH? IMMORTALISTS AND ENTREPRENEURS

Will there be a cure for death in your lifetime? I won't even parse the built-in paradox in that sentence, but I will give you an answer to the question, upfront. The answer is *maybe*. Now that may seem disappointingly vague, but the mere fact that the answer is not *no,* is amazing.

In fact, there's a group of Silicon Valley entrepreneurs mad on the heels of a solution. Why? Because they are getting older. After all Gates and even Zuckerberg are no longer spring chickens. Baby Boomers, as they near the finish line, are particularly interested in this subject. Peter Thiel, the tech billionaire, is after it, as is Jeff Bezos. Since Bezos has a shot at being the first-ever trillionaire, money is not an object. Google has even invested a billion and a half dollars in their Calico Longevity Lab. There are even venture capitalists and established foundations focused solely on longevity engineering, a cure for death.

"Death makes me very angry . . . It doesn't make any sense to me. Death has never made any sense to me. How can a person be there and then just vanish, just not be there?"
  – Larry Ellison, CEO of Oracle Corporation

Why is this happening now? I mean people have been chasing the elusive "Fountain of Youth" since Ponce de Leon. It's all in the genes. The understanding of genetics is evolving at an astonishing pace. I was born before Watson and Crick had discovered the double-helix, and today you can do gene hacking yourself in the kitchen. Some current research is focused on telomeres, the protein caps on chromosomes that protect them from aging. Elizabeth Blackburn won the Nobel in 2009 for her work on telomeres. Other research, like at the Salk Institute, has had some success reversing epigenetic changes in mice and human embryos. The researchers, by reprogramming genes, have not only been able to slow aging but to reverse it. Bingo!

Please understand that none of these dreamers and innovators ignore the fact, even if successful, body parts wear out, cancer strikes, or strokes appear in the night. But a cure for death: would living to 150 at least be so bad? The jury's out on that one. What do you think?

Meanwhile, is it hubris or vanity that drives the longevity entrepreneurs? I'd contend that it takes a certain amount of hubris and vanity to believe you can achieve the impossible, or at least do something that's never been done before. Take Elon Musk. Spaceship to Mars, why not? Power 40,000 homes in Australia with solar and batteries for free, sure. Build a car company worth more than General Motors, piece of cake. Well not really. These big accomplishments require vision, resources, and a lot of hard work. The Silicon Valley girls and boys have all three.

Now I think there may be a viable, if not better, path to immortality. That is to transfer your brain, emotions, and personality to the cloud. The reason it may be better is that computer servers, especially with backups, are more durable media than our bodies. If we were truly able to capture the essence of our beings and upload them, we could live a pretty full life digitally forever. There is plenty of research and progress being made on this parallel course.

"In time, you will discover ways to move your mind to more durable media."

– Nick Bostrom, Director – Future of Humanity Institute

Some of my friends think I might be pretty obsessed with the subject of a *cure for death*. Maybe because I did spend three years writing my thriller novel, *Not So Dead* on the subject, but I can't think of a bigger puzzle to solve. Can you?

QUESTIONOLOGY: THE POWERFUL
SCIENCE OF GREAT QUESTIONS

Why do I find good questions so powerful and fascinating? Makes sense to start an essay about questions with a question, right? It's because of what just happened in your brain when you read those first two sentences. You may not realize it consciously, but your subconscious automatically engages to try to answer those questions. You can't help it. So your brain tried but could not answer the first question, since you don't know me and why I find anything fascinating.

To the second question, you probably answered subconsciously, *Yes,* because you had all the information you needed to answer. So the first question is still a bit of a puzzle for you, maybe makes you even a little uneasy but hopefully makes you want to read further. The second question is maybe a bit more satisfying because you could answer it, but already your subconscious has detected a pattern and is beginning to surmise what this essay is about: Questionology.

So if you're still reading, those first two questions were very good questions, weren't they? They engaged you, got you thinking, maybe made you curious and wanting to know more. That's the power of good questions and part of why I find good questions so fascinating.

Let me tell you a story. I have done a lot of public speaking and teaching in my career in the areas of decision-making and technology. I noticed very early on, when I was giving a seminar to a corporate group of twenty, that when I just spoke in declarative sentences, their eyes glazed over. A good public speaker is always checking to see if their audience is still tuned in. However, if I started asking questions, they perked up and paid attention. I wondered why that was? Then I began to realize that we cannot resist or tune out questions, can we? Whether we like it or not, when faced with a question, our subconscious will automatically engage to try to answer. You and I have no conscious control over this response, do we?

Now I owe you the rest of the story. The group I was addressing was in the business of manufacturing gunpowder. So when one of my questions to them was, "What qualifications do you need to work here?"

A young woman answered, "You need to be able to run fast."

Now I was getting curious and asked the all-important follow-up question. "Why? Why do you need to be able to run fast?"

She replied, "Because we have lots of explosions in the plant, and you need to be able to get out of the way, fast."

True story. Often the answers you get back from your questions are unexpected, aren't they?

The second most powerful thing you can do in communicating in addition to asking good questions is to tell stories. We love stories, don't we? Why is that? I think it's either built into our human nature or something we learn as kids or maybe both. But that's a subject for another essay. Back to questions.

When I began to come to grips with the power of questions, I did a little experiment. In one of my seminars, I talked about the power of questions to solve problems. But for thirty minutes of my presentation on this topic, I phrased every sentence in the form of a question. What do you think happened? Did their heads explode? No, but something magical happened. They got the point. How often does that happen?

So over the last twenty years, as part of my fascination with questions, I have been collecting good and great questions whenever I heard or read them. Kinda crazy, right? What I began to find is that some questions not only engaged your mind but also had the power to redirect your actions and in many cases, change your life.

As an aside, I will mention that I became so enamored with the power of good questions, that I have made a study of them. In fact, I coined the term Questionology in 2009. If you enjoy and benefit from the power of these questions, you will be able to learn more, see and discuss good questions in my blog at Questionology.com (coming soon). Bits and pieces of helpful things have been written about good questions, but I'd like to see it pulled together in one cohesive place. That's one of *my* definitions of success. I envision that someday, the art and science of questions will be taught in school, although Socrates may have beat me to it by a few years. Can you picture a day when you'll be able to get a degree in Questionology? I can. Let's get started.

Here's your first potentially life-changing question:

What's your definition of success?

The keyword here is *your*. It's personal to you. You may want to think about it for a little, but I'll tweak your thinking a bit first. Success can be small like achieving the goals in a project you're responsible for. Or bigger, at the end of your life, how would you define success? Making a lot of money, raising a great family, inspiring or helping others? Based on your answer, would you change what you are doing now, today or tomorrow? Is what you spend your time on contributing to your definition of success? Good questions, right? The kinds of questions that have the power to create change. Would you agree?

SECRET SURVEILLANCE. IS THE EYE IN THE SKY WATCHING YOU?

I magine this. An armed robbery takes place. Men in masks with shotguns pull up in a white van to the 1st National Bank. Three get out, enter the bank, and shots are fired. Ninety seconds later they exit the bank and speed off. It's two minutes before the police arrive and the robbers are long gone. What's to be done?

Now, what if the police department had every step of this crime recorded? And even further, they could rewind, like your DVR, and see where the men set out from and their faces before they donned the masks. Then they could fast forward and see where they dumped the white van, changed vehicles, and where they are right now. "It's almost like the police have a time machine!" Sounds like surveillance science fiction? It's happening now.

While doing research for my thriller novel, *NOT SO DEAD*, I came across just the technology described above called Persistent Surveillance ("PS"). PS is the brainchild of Ross McNutt, Air Force Academy graduate, physicist, and MIT-trained astronautical engineer who in 2004 founded the Air Force's Center for Rapid Product Development.

"It's almost like the police have a time machine!"

In *NOT SO DEAD,* Homeland Security tracks my fictional terrorist in New York City. In real life, the Baltimore, Maryland, and Dayton, Ohio, police departments have used Persistent Surveillance to track criminals from start to finish in the commission of crimes. PS actually tracks all activity out in the open on every street in the city for which it is deployed within a five-mile radius. In Baltimore, they covered thirty-two miles. So any crime that takes place in the open can be tracked past present and future to its inevitable arrest and conclusion.

PS uses light aircraft circling over a city 24/7 to watch and record all activities on every street. Unlike traditional satellite surveillance where the camera is taking pinhole video, the mounted cameras on the PS aircraft take wide-area images. Then using hi-tech software that stitches the images together, operators are able to piece together the string of activities that take place on the recordings from start to finish.

How widespread is the use of persistent surveillance? Right now more because of politics and cost, it is only being used in a few cities on a test basis. But McNutt's hope and vision is that it becomes more widespread. He bet the farm on it when he founded Persistent Surveillance Systems. Are there opportunities for abuse and invasion of privacy? Certainly, you could imagine that scenario, but is the radical lowering of crime and protection of citizens worth it? That's the constant quandary and paradox of new technologies, like Persistent Surveillance, as they are designed and tested to protect our citizens. What do you think?

CAN YOU GROW YOUR OWN COMPUTER? BIOLOGICAL COMPUTING IS HERE

I n a recent essay, we talked about the quantum leap of Quantum Computers. They can potentially do extremely complex problem-solving hundreds of times faster than today's fastest supercomputers. The only problem is that you have to house them in giant refrigerators and freeze them to—272 degrees Fahrenheit. The environmental constraints are so demanding and the process so fragile that accuracy can become a problem.

So this nascent, but possibly game-changing, technology won't be inside your cell phone anytime soon. However, what if we could harness the ultra-fast, mini-miracles of the processes that take place in biological cells at normal temperatures to perform complex and daunting computer tasks? Yes, use biology to make fifth-generation computers. Biological computing is happening now. Read on.

As we discussed in the post on Quantum Computing, traditional computers are sequential thinkers, 1s and 0s. Quantum Computers and now biological computers can do parallel processing. This is what enables big gains in speed. If you think about the cells in your body, they don't wait for one thing to happen, then another, then another after that. No! Millions of processes are happening in your body *simultaneously* right now. Biological computers can harness that massive parallel processing power to do complex calculations and solve big data problems at lightning speed.

Researchers from Lund University in Sweden have produced prototype biological computers that do calculations many times faster than traditional computers. They have produced a working proof of concept. The biological computer uses nanotechnology in the form of cells, generally implanted in bacteria, like e.coli.

"In simple terms, it involves the building of a labyrinth of nano-based channels that have specific traffic regulations for protein filaments. The solution in the labyrinth corresponds to the answer of a mathematical question, and many molecules can find their way through the labyrinth at the same time", says Heiner Linke, director of NanoLund and coordinator of the parallel computer study. Using this parallel computing approach, Lund scientists were able to take a classic problem, the "Subset Sum Problem," and solve it in a drastically shorter time than traditional sequential computing.

Someday the powers of nanobiotechnology may take us beyond computers. I often think of the great sci-fi book *The Unreasoning Mask* by Philip Jose Farmer where our hero flies in a biological spaceship. It's actually alive and responsive while being an amazing spaceship.

It gets even cooler because this technology is cheap. Why? Because you can grow the cells or essentially grow the computer in a Petri dish! It's also cheap because it consumes very little energy. I mean think about it. Your brain is currently running thousands, if not millions, of processes and all you need is a few Oreos and you're good to go. Check that. You may need some potato chips and coffee too.

Compare biocomputers to quantum computers that require expensive, large refrigerators walled-off from all magnetic fields and huge amounts of power. The economics and practicality of biological computers may win the race to providing the high-speed parallel processing machines and devices of the future.

For now, this technology is at the baby stage, but expectations are that in ten years it may be commercially available and maybe it will actually be in your cell phone someday.

DO-IT-YOURSELF GENE HACKING –
GOOD, BAD, UGLY, AND SCARY

W hat if someone could buy all the genetic engineering tools and materials for a few hundred dollars online to develop a cure for a disease or start a plague? Science fiction, right? Nope. You can now order your gene hacking supplies at Odin.com to get started. New gene hacking tools, including the powerful CRISPR/Cas9, allow amateurs and professionals alike to dive into DNA with GPS-like accuracy and then remove, add, and modify genes. For those who love acronyms, CRISPR stands for "Clustered Regularly Interspaced Short Palindromic Repeats."

While curing a disease or creating anthrax-like viruses is not that simple, with these new and evolving tools, the possibilities are there for far faster and affordable research, development, and deployment of genetically based mutations and products--products that could have a significant potential impact on our everyday lives.

First, Gene Hacking – Good News

Rapid development of altered-genetic materials, using this readily available CRISPR technology, could soon lead to major advances:

1> **Drugs and therapies**—to cure cancer, heart disease, blindness, and eventually more genetically complex diseases like diabetes and multiple sclerosis.

2> **Organ transplants**—make possible pig organ transplants by removing pig retroviruses, making the transplants safer for humans.

3> **Remove insect-born diseases**—like malaria from mosquitoes or SARS from bats.

4> **Create Super Plants**—some are now being developed at Rutgers using CRISPR to resist mildew and other pathogens.

5> **Edit human embryos**—to remove genetic dispositions to diseases like leukemia and breast cancer.

Second, Gene Hacking – Bad News

1> **Terrorism**—gene editing tools in the wrong hands open the possibility for genetically modified viruses to be developed and deployed. That may be why intelligence agencies have expressed concern that the "broad distribution, low cost and accelerated pace of development" of these genetic tools may lead to "deliberate or unintentional misuse that might further lead to far-reaching economic and national security implications."

Further, these tools could be used to attack crops and livestock with either genetically modified chemicals or insects.

2> **Hacking**—now this may sound even crazier, but researchers at the University of Washington have shown that software edited into a genetic sequence can create a different kind of virus. It's a virus that does not infect humans, but when run through a gene-sequencer for analysis it actually infects the computer of the analyzer and can take over that computer and its healthcare network—presumably for control by its malicious creator.

Like all new technology from the transcontinental railroad to computers to the Internet, it brings great wonders and gifts to society along with opportunities for malice and abuse. Over time, great societies have worked on multiple levels to amplify the good aspects and minimize the bad. The keyword here is 'Time." Governments and institutions need time to understand and try to "get ahead" of the opportunities and challenges of new scientific developments. The problem with DIY gene hacking, like recent advances in artificial intelligence, is that the developments and abuses are coming much faster than our ability to cope with the changes or threats they present.

The conclusion is that we may need a Manhattan-like

project to understand and cope with the changes this rapidly evolving world of genetic science offers . . . before it's too late.

Meanwhile, maybe I'll order a CRISPR kit online for research purposes. Maybe I can reverse the aging gene for the sequel I'm writing to *STILL NOT DEAD*.

WHERE'VE YOU BEEN?

Yesterday, I was struck by a friend's Facebook post that linked to a video of a Grammy-winning song, a standout from a relatively unknown artist—at least unknown to me. My friend warned me that I'd need to have tissues on hand. He was right; I cried my eyes out.

After I pulled myself together, I had to ask the big "Why" question: *why* did I have such a visceral reaction to the song?

Before reading on, you might want to watch the video yourself. On YouTube, search for *"Where've You Been* by Don Henry" to view it.

If you felt as I did, then the song had emotional resonance for you. But why? For most of us, the books, songs, movies, and art that sticks with us well beyond the reading, listening, or viewing, are works that go to the heart, not the head. The resonance seems to start with something in the DNA of the narrative that is genuinely authentic for us, words, images or a melody that we know are true. In my case, I've been married to the love of my life for decades. Or maybe it's because I lost my father at too young an age and my mother to suicide. So it seems the notions of love and loss struck a powerful responsive chord with me. Then there's the song title, "Where've You Been." As you heard in the video, songwriter Don Henry heard those actual words spoken by his grandmother to her near-to-death husband of sixty years. As listeners, we know that somebody actually uttered those poignant words at a transcendent moment. We know it's true deep in our gut that at some time we all lose the people most near and dear to us…a reminder that we need to make the most of our time with them, rather than looking back with regrets.

Then there's the question of the question embedded in the title "Where've You Been." *That's* a big one. In an earlier essay, *Questionology: The Powerful Science of Great Questions*, I talked about how great questions tap into our souls and demand a verbal or emotional response. In the case of listening to the song, for me, the response was a wellspring of sentimental tears. There's also an appealing ambiguity to that question, *Where've You Been*. It could mean, "Where'd you go while you were away from me?" "Where have you been all my life?" "What's been your life's journey?" "Are you somewhere else and will you come back to me?" Choose one or write your own. We fit the question to our own personal experiences.

So we have authentic words uttered and a powerful question. What's the glue that brings it all together? I believe it's the story so beautifully and briefly told in the lyrics and amplified by Henry's pre-amble that gives us a glimpse into his creative process. I'm endlessly fascinated by the power of stories to draw us into another place, another world, and alter our emotional states. Maybe that's why I became a writer—I love to read, watch, and tell stories. If you ever do public speaking or even just converse with friends and you say, "Let me tell you a story," you will grab their attention immediately. We all want to hear a story, to be entertained, to be taken beyond ourselves.

Finally, there is transcendence, the rare and wondrous experience of listening to a story that combines all the elements mentioned above. It's a Gestalt in which the whole becomes greater than the sum of the parts, and the resulting magic elevates us to another plane. After a few refrains of *Where've You Been*, you're immersed in the life story of a long-married couple—how they met, their life together, and the final eternal binding of their souls. I can name several, and yet too few, creative works that have had a similar effect on me. Those that transcend all seem to contain emotionally real words, a question, a well-told story, and some indescribable magic. That's why they win Grammys, Oscars, and Pulitzers and somehow, we all know why deep in our gut.

WHAT'S IN A NAME?

S am *Sunborn* is the hero in my *NOT SO DEAD thriller series*. Readers ask, "Where'd that name come from?" The quick answer is I dreamed it up, but there is really more to it. Names are important and personal, aren't they? In fiction, they may take on more levels of meaning and even be a precious gift to readers. They can be symbolic (think *Luke Skywalker*), clever (*Katniss Everdeen)*, humorous: (*Holly Golightly)*, and ironic (*Maxwell Smart*). A good name when associated with a memorable character can even transcend the book to become part of the daily lexicon (think "Rambo").

"Sam's unique name helps. He even has his own Twitter account."

Names continually fascinate me, both in the real world and in literature. Readers of my newsletter may remember the fun we had with aptronyms—actual names that sometimes humorously reflect people's professions like Dr. Timothy Kneebone, Chiropractor, or Dr. Benjamin Leak, Urologist.

In writing *NOT SO DEAD*, I wanted a name that was memorable, symbolic, euphonic, and unique. What does that mean?

Memorable doesn't just mean easy to remember. The name should have some resonance, teasing something in your subconscious. Among readers, *Sam Sunborn* seems to have some kind of ethereal connection to famous characters like Jason Bourne or Sam Seaborn. Good.

Symbolic. The meaning of the name reflects the character's personality and actions. *Sunborn* equals *born of the sun.* Like Apollo, he radiates light, optimism, and power. Although he frequently fails, he tries to illuminate most of the time.

Short. If the name's too long, you probably won't remember it. Michael Connelly fans know *Bosch*—short, punchy, but most wouldn't remember his full name, *Hieronymous Bosch,* and Connelly only occasionally mentions that long first name.

Euphonic. Names that sound good stick with us. If I say, *Serena*, you'll probably know who I'm referring to. The name *Serena* just flows like a wave and is pleasant to say and to hear. Further, alliteration lends some poetry to a name like *Marilyn Monroe* (real person, made-up name). In *Sam Sunborn,* you have the repetitive *S.* I also like the one-syllable first name and the two-syllable last name—it's kind of like a jab then a punch, a *da-ta-ta.*

Unique. Although the name *Sam Sunborn* is short and simple, it is totally unique. That's intentional. Not only does it hold a singular place in memory, but if you Google *Sam Sunborn*, he dominates the results—every Google entry is a reference to my Sam in one of the *NOT SO DEAD* books, on

Amazon, Goodreads, Audible, Apple, Twitter, and more. As an author, I do like to sell books. Sam's unique name helps. He even has his own Twitter account. You can follow him @SamSunborn.

What about all the supporting character names? The other type of names that seems to resonate with readers are authentic, actual names. Can't you tell when a name sounds real from when it sounds fake? That's why most of the other characters in my most recent thrillers *NOT SO DONE* and *STILL NOT DEAD* are the true names of my readers. Huh? Yes, in the last two summers, I asked for volunteers, *Who wants to be murdered in my next book?* Over two hundred good-humored readers raised a hand, and many of them will have the pleasure of seeing their names in my pages—both good guys and villainous men and women.

So what's in a name? Maybe more than you think.

THE TROUBLE WITH THE ON BUTTON

"Findability precedes usability. In the alphabet and on the Web. You can't use what you can't find." — Peter Morville

I wouldn't have brought this up unless I noticed a pattern. First, let me explain that I am not a tech novice. In fact, I have run a technology consulting company for twenty-six years and I've always been the go-to, fix-it guy in my family. But recently I have been stumped trying to find the *ON* button and dealing with some previously simple electronic tasks. How about you?

Let me give you two examples. First, take the new laptop I recently purchased for its speed and power to replace my older, clunkier machine. In my business career, I have probably owned a dozen laptop computers going back to my 1981 Osborne 1 (Pre-PC) with two giant floppy disks. And in all those years, I never had a problem finding the *ON* button. However, when I cracked open my brand-new Dell laptop last week, it was nowhere to be found!

Usually, a laptop has a power button above or to the right side of the keyboard. It's not there. *Where's the power button?*

Not finding the button in the usual places, I turned the new machine over and checked the sides and the back. No button. To get the darn thing started, I found a workaround online where you press CTRL + ESC keys and plug in the power cord at the same time. That worked, so I could perform the typical twenty-two steps to set up Windows 10. The laptop is great, and I love it, *but there's got to be an ON button*, I thought.

Since my new laptop did not come with a user manual or

directions, typical these days, I searched online first for the exact Dell model number. Guess what? It showed a clear diagram of the keyboard with a separate power button that does not actually exist on my version of the very same model. So I called Dell support. Once reached a human, it took their tech several minutes of research to finally point out that the button was indeed the top right *unmarked* black key mixed in with the other keys on the keyboard. It didn't even show the power symbol (the little circle with a vertical line through it).

Oh, and I learned that the unidentified key is the fingerprint reader too. Even a fingerprint symbol on that key would be helpful. How intuitive--not. Why would they make the most basic and simple step of owning and using a laptop so confusing? I will share my theory momentarily.

Example #2. I would have let the laptop *ON* button escapade pass, but then another wonky thing happened when I tried using a new chainsaw for the first time to handle the ongoing tree issues around our house. I probably have hundreds of trees in the woods that make up most of our property and occasionally they fall across the lawn, the driveway, and unfortunately, on the power lines. In case you think I'm exaggerating about the trees, see the picture below of my trees that came down on power lines during Hurricane Sandy. They blocked traffic for two weeks until the power company got around to us.

So you either own a chainsaw and handle the issues yourself or get a second mortgage to provide room and board for a tree surgeon. After owning several gas chainsaws, I learned the beauty and pleasure of the newer electric chainsaws that seem to have all the power without the noise and the frustration of yanking on a starter cord. I tested this alternative by buying a small electric chainsaw from Green-Works last year. It worked beautifully, with very little hassle. So I bought the larger model to handle bigger trees this year. I got it this past spring but was so busy with work and writing and painting some columns outside my house I didn't have time to use it until yesterday. It looks exactly like the smaller chainsaw in color, green naturally, and design but has a larger battery and a bigger saw blade. After assembling it, I put in the chainsaw oil, pressed the same two buttons—the safety, and the trigger—and nothing. What? My first thought was that there is no way I will be able to return or get this replaced if it's defective after all this time. I checked the user manual. No enlightenment there. With some careful inspection, I spotted a subtly camouflaged *ON* button. The smaller saw of similar design from the same company didn't require any such button. I pressed that newly discovered button, then the safety and trigger. To my relief, it kicked in with a pleasant whir and no smell of gasoline.

Am I just a complainer or is there a pattern here? I could go on with other examples like the printer cartridge that wouldn't fit in my HP printer and don't get me started on shrink wrap and child safety caps on medicine bottles. Pardon my rant, but these occurrences are particularly frustrating for someone like me to whom others have looked to fix their broken items, open stuck bottles, and solve almost any mechanical or electrical problem over the years. If Mr. Fixit is having these problems, I can imagine what the average user must be encountering.

OK, why is this happening now? Let's charitably assume I don't have early onset dementia and am thereby not losing it. It's an iffy assumption, but let's go with it for the moment. I believe the more likely scenario has to do with product designers making assumptions without regard to usability, i.e. how you and I will use these things. It's what usability engineers (yes, that's a real science and profession) call the *User Experience* or UX. Remember when things you purchased came with detailed user manuals that included diagrams and step-by-step instructions? Not anymore. I think the beginning of the decline started when companies opted to make their devices "intuitive" to use or made the user go online to try to figure things out. To some degree, they were successful. For example, most Google software makes it easy to figure out which buttons to push when you want to do something. Youtube is also very helpful with How-Tos. Yet as theirs and other companies' products evolve and get more complicated with more options and more choices for the user to make, usability suffers—things break down.

The second reason I believe things are harder to use is they're replacing English with icons. The ostensible reason for replacing "ON" with the circle and vertical bar sticking out the top is the limited space on a single small button or keyboard key—really? How much space does "ON" take up? So the usability engineers assume everybody knows what the circle/bar and other cryptic shapes mean. Still, I know people, many dear to me, who don't know what the circle/bar signifies or even the > or >> or || mean on their remote controls of DVD players or that three dots or four horizontal lines on their iPhone apps indicate tap-to-see-the-menu. Apparently, Dell has taken it a step further into the abyss—a blank, black key now means *ON*. Don't believe me? See the figure below.

So here's a shout-out or more like a cry-out to all the

gifted companies and their usability engineers who create the products and UX that are supposed to make our lives *easier* every day. Give us a real user manual, separate the *ON* button from the other buttons, and put "ON" on it. While you're at it, cut out the shrink wrap and childproof caps. That will truly make our lives easier and, over time, give us years of our lives back.

Are you with me on this?

IN THE BIRD'S EYE

*I*s there a sea of souls out there just waiting to be placed in *bodies? Does the Golem of Kabbalah lore, a man-beast with a mismatched soul, truly exist?* These are questions I ask myself while I stroll down 5th Avenue in the pandemic ghost town formerly known as New York City, USA. The famous stores are boarded up and the street is empty with only the occasional vacant yellow cab passing by. Men and women sleep hidden under newspapers in doorways. *Could I be them? Could they be me?* It seems like I'm a lost soul from a dystopian future who now occupies this well-worn male body.

It's autumn with the remaining trees planted decades ago popping up through the concrete, shedding their orange and yellow leaves in slow motion. Where is the street vendor and that bold, sweet smell of chestnuts roasting on the corner of 56th? Am I the only one who feels disconnected from this new reality? I walk north to Central Park, which is still an oasis amidst the big city. The crisp cool air in the park is cleaner and clearer, lacking both pre-pandemic pollution and noise. Maybe that's why there are so many more birds chattering in the trees and picking through twigs in the meadow.

Further on, a doting mother and a child, a small girl with curly blonde hair in a Raggedy-Ann costume dress, sit on a blanket. They pick at french fries from a plastic container. An old man in a still older wool coat and fedora occupies the far side of a bench, reading a magazine. The near side of the bench beckons with the promise of rest and more pleasant meditation on the day. Taking a seat, I slip the thick paperback of *The Odyssey* from my backpack, the story never complete, mysteries and nuance always unfolding, the rhythm and patter soothing. But not this time. This body is too restless. The muscles in the legs and back beg to move. The mind rejects the written word in favor of the songs of fall, the wind, the trees, the people. I'm up again, ambling the winding path to nowhere in particular.

Shadows pass beneath my feet. I flinch, then look up to see migrating redtail hawks flying in formation overhead. They interrupt the sunlight to awaken a primordial wariness from which my ancient soul recoils by instinct. The majestic predators land in a nearby glowing red Japanese maple, resting before the next big leg of their journey over water to Staten Island. There are a few bikers and walkers here fighting the tide of loneliness and lethargy that has swept through the city, the country, the world. What is the answer? What is their answer? I turn my head and cock my ear to listen. And a soft whisper comes back to me, floating on the

carpet of a gentle breeze. Their simple, succinct clue to living and surviving with this strange soul in this foreign body is...
"Take hope. Keep going. The journey that stirs you now is not far off."

-END-

LIKED THE LAST APPOINTMENT?

Liked *The Last Appointment?*

Check out more adventures of Sam, Michelle, Rich and Al in the *NOT SO DEAD Series* or the *NOT SO DEAD Trilogy* by Charles Levin.

If you enjoyed *The Last Appointment*, please consider leaving an unbiased review on Amazon, Goodreads, or Bookbub to help spread the word.

You can learn more about this book and the author at www.charleslevin.com

Contact or follow the author at

Contact: charleslevin.com/contact

Facebook: facebook.com/Charles.Levin.Author

Instagram: @charleslevinauthor

Bookbub: bookbub.com/authors/charles-levin

Goodreads: goodreads.com/author/show/18896291.Charles_Levin

ACKNOWLEDGMENTS

Many thanks to my readers who commented in my blog, shared their Moonlanding memories, answered my casting call for Who wants to be murdered in my next book? (hundreds of you volunteered), and posted thoughtful and enthusiastic reviews. Without you my cherished readers, this crazy writing passion of mine wouldn't be nearly as much fun or as gratifying. You keep me going.

And then there are the usual suspects to thank for putting my manuscript in order--my editors Judy Roth and Gabriella Swartwood as well as my dear friend and sounding board, Steve Bennett.

A final thanks to my wife Amy for her unflagging support and my two sons to whom this collection is dedicated.

ABOUT THE AUTHOR

Charlie is an author who has written, in addition to this short story collection, four thriller novels, NOT SO DEAD, NOT SO GONE, NOT SO DONE, and STILL NOT DEAD. Charlie's 26-year background in tech, degree in philosophy, and love of fast-paced thrillers are the brew that created them.

He lives in New Jersey with his wife, Amy, and has two sons, too far away in California.

EXCERPT FROM STILL NOT DEAD, THE LATEST SAM SUNBORN THRILLER

Chapter 1 — Memories Lost

Monica stands motionless in the vestibule, her arms extended and curled as if still hugging the suddenly vanished body of her husband. The warmth and gentleness of his touch like a phantom limb, almost there, but not.

"Mom, Mom!" Evan cries from the steps. "What's going on, what happened?"

Her back to Evan, Monica lets her arms drop to her side. She straightens her skirt. With both hands, she pulls her hair back, forces a smile, and turns to him. "Your father left." She sniffs. "He'll be back soon."

"No, he won't," Evan says. "He's dead again, isn't he?"

Monica hesitates. She doesn't know what to say.

"You're a liar. Dad's a liar. You're both liars and now he's gone." Evan turns and stomps back up the steps, his footfalls echoing like gunshots.

* * *

When you fade away, what's left? The last thing I remember was my arms wrapped around Monica, her energy, the fragrance of her lavender perfume, our dog Petey barking at my return, Evan running down the steps to greet me. And then it happened. I'm not sure if it was gradual or like flash paper, but I disappeared, gone.

"Where's Dad?" Evan said, and that's the last thing I remember.

Now, where am I? I'm not sure—it's pitch-black and quiet like outer space. Feeling, I cannot. Then what am I? A thought floating like a feather in a cloud? I'm not sure. How would I know? Don't thoughts and feelings need to be attached to something, like something physical, a brain, a body? Apparently not. I'm not sure how long I can go on like this. Do I have a choice? It's as if they buried me alive, but I will not run out of air. Seems I don't need air. That's right—I'm not breathing. Is this what death is like? Am I dead again? I'm convinced it's not a dream.

Wait, I hear something. It's faint, like the sound of crinkling paper, but far away. It's getting closer, louder. Something's burning. Ooh, now it's gone. Then, a high-pitched tone, like a high C. It's getting louder. Now it's fading again. No tongue, yet I taste salt, so salty. The memory of salt?

Dead silent again, and still dark. Something tells me to breathe, but I can't.

A flash of light as if I can see through my closed eyelids.

... For more, look for STILL NOT DEAD on Amazon or BarnesAndNoble.com

Made in the USA
Middletown, DE
04 December 2021